SECRET OF METAL

The Elementals Book 5

Jennifer L. Kelly

This is a work of fiction. All of the characters, organizations, and events portrayed in this novel are either products of the author's imagination or are used fictitiously.

Library of Congress PCN: 2017913618

BoxerBull Books

Cleveland, OH

ISBN-10: 0-9977764-9-8

ISBN-13: 978-0-9977764-9-2

IF YOU THOUGHT BEING ORDINARY WAS A BAD
THING, THINK AGAIN.
-J.L.K.

OTHER BOOKS BY JENNIFER L. KELLY

THE ELEMENTALS

ARMY OF FIRE
THE EARTH KEY
GENESIS OF WOOD
THE WATER QUEEN

THE LUCIA CHRONICLES

THE PROPHECY
THE DISSENTIENT
THE BEACON
THE GIRL WHO WASN'T LOVED (NOVELLA)

STAND ALONE FICTION

THE FRACTURED LIFE OF JENNY MCCLAIN

PROLOGUE

It wasn't supposed to be this way. Li was never supposed to get hurt. He was never supposed to be drained of his Fire. My mom and dad should both still be here. But they're not. And Ahna. Ahna wasn't supposed to die. But she did.

If I was feeling exceptionally sorry for myself, I'd say that it was all my fault. Maybe it is. But in my heart I know that it isn't. My mom always said, "Head or heart, Kata?" Well, I said heart. And my heart says none of this is my fault. It's the fault of the Imminent Darkness.

What's the Imminent Darkness you ask? It's an ancient, evil force that seeks to restore balance to the Universe. The ID's MO is deception, torture, and murder. A long time ago five sisters—goddesses of the Universe—were tricked by an old codger, the Imminent Darkness in disguise. Long story short, he created rivalry between the sisters and each one was given a stone. An Elemental stone. Because the sisters could no longer get along, their parents Raj and Katayun—King and Queen of the Universe respectively, and also my grandparents—created a land for each of the daughters to inhabit. One each for Earth, Water, Wood, Fire, and Metal. My mother, Novea, ruled the Land of Earth. Eventually, she came to live on Xon 9 and fell in love with a mortal man, my dad, Absalom. One thing led to another as these things tend to do, and they had me. Thing is, there's no one else like me in the universe. My mother's sisters gifted me with the Elemental stones upon my birth, and in so doing a part of each Element. But that was a very dangerous thing to do. Soon, I was showing aptitude at a young age for each Element. Which, naturally, just wouldn't do because here on Xon 9 you get to choose one and only one Element.

So what's a mother to do? She consulted an old Metal woman with the Sight. The Seer kept the stones safe for a while, but eventually she gave them back to my mother to throw into the Elemental Abyss. It was an act to protect me. Only, it has had the complete opposite effect. Because eventually I found out who—or what—I truly am. I am the Impossible Girl. I am all possibilities and yet I am none.

The Imminent Darkness is taking over my planet. It has hurt many people that I love. It killed my best friend. And its human minions have terrorized the colonists of Xon 9. Power is the reward. Fear is the currency. But no more. I will retrieve the Elemental stones and restore what's rightfully mine. I feel the pulse of Earth in my veins. The electricity of Fire in my blood. I have gained the wisdom of Wood, more than any normal teenager should have to bear when she should be thinking about boys and University, instead of saving the world. The gentle ferocity of Water fuels my spirit. Five stones. Four retrieved and destroyed. One left to go.

CHAPTER 1

I kick at the wall again. Pushing my soft-padded shoes against the steel wall. The bed is stiff and feels like plywood. The aches in my back subsided long ago. An agonizing scream echoes off the metal walls of the hallway. I close my eyes and listen to the pad of boots trotting down the hallway. Being here, in this cell, my senses all seem heightened.

The room is stark. Everything is stainless steel. The walls, the door, the ceiling, the toilet. Everything but the bed. When I close my eyes, I can hear the self-assured step of the Metal soldiers as they walk around. They're trained to run and barely make a sound, but if I close my eyes and the whiteness fills my head, then I can hear them. I've even come to identify some of their steps. The heavy-footed stride of the red-haired soldier. The toe-to-heal stride of the blonde with a penchant for sharp objects. The soft-scraping of the sound of Michaela's boots.

She doesn't know that I know. But even in the dark, I can see. Her blonde hair, stripped of its luster. The chapped bottom lip from biting it so often over whether or not she did the right thing. She's sure she did the right thing. I can hear her as she presses her palm flush against the door and then presses her forehead against its coolness. The slight rattle of her breath. Because she doesn't know what I already know. That it's only a matter of time before the entire colony is infected. Before what killed my best friend, kills them too. But I'm safe here in my little metal cocoon. Safe from the world outside. Michaela doesn't care that she betrayed me. But she does care that she betrayed her brother. She lifts her forehead from the door and I can almost see the resolution in those steely blue eyes, her hand curling into a fist.

She had no choice. I was a threat to the Leadership Council. It had to be done. The image of an old, now blind man drifts into her mind, like cobwebs long-forgotten in the corners. Did he deserve his punishment for speaking out against the Leadership Council? She shakes her head as if the cobwebs could fall out of her ears and onto the steel floor, where she grinds them beneath the heal of her black, military-issued combat boots. She was trained to uphold the law. But is the law always so black and white?

The glare of the light reflects off the web of silvery, metallic threads that line the right side of her face. She sighs softly. Again, the faintest of rattles. And I hear the soft scrape of her boots as she continues down the hallway, resigned to live with the choices she's made.

There's no sense of time in a cell with no windows. I lost track of the days long ago. I know I'm awake more than I sleep. My eyes feel as if they're full of sand. My almost shoulder length brown hair is knotted and greasy. I don't eat the food they give me. Well, besides the rock-hard bread. They can keep their mystery meat and so-called vegetable melody. More like vegetable catastrophe. I've lost weight. If I run my fingers over my jumpsuit and over my waist, I can count my ribs individually. What would Sloan say if he saw me now? I kick at the wall again. It makes a soft, muffled sound.

My chest feels constricted whenever I think about Sloan, as if my heart is trying to claw its way out and up my throat. Tears no longer sting the backs of my eyes when I think of him. I know it hasn't been that long, but has it been long enough? Those sea-green eyes and shaggy brown hair, beautiful silvery-green scales that used to line the side of his face, like the sea come to life. That's my Sloan. Assuming he's still mine. He is. My heart knows it. My head hopes it. But he hasn't visited me in my dreams. Neither has his mom, Bina.

The worst part of being in here is the not-doing. The Imminent Darkness is out there, creeping through the Elemental Abyss, its darkness seeping into the nooks and crannies of my home. The only home I've ever known. And I'm locked in here for no crime, except doing what I know is right and asking the questions no one wants to ask. The Imminent Darkness is feeding on the energy of the inhabitants of Xon 9, growing stronger as it devours their souls. And there's not a damn thing I can do about it.

There's a loud click. The sound of the keypad being accessed to open my cell. The door slides open and a tall, red-haired guy with a neck as big as my waist enters. The door slides closed behind him. He wears all black and has a gun holstered on his belt. His uniform is meticulous. The garish lighting causes the right side of his face to appear in a soft blur of silver. It's the heavy-footed soldier arrived with my dinner—or breakfast—one can never tell.

"Dinner, Number 8392." He sets the tray at the foot of the bed and takes a step back. I slide myself upright and swing my legs around so they're no longer against the wall. I don't answer. I never answer.

Officer Red Hair doesn't appear much older than me. I'm eighteen and I peg him for maybe Sloan's age, twenty-two. Most likely he's only been in this position for a couple of moons. He crosses his arms and cuts me a glare, hazel eyes narrowed.

"Are you planning on starving yourself to death?"

"It would be quicker," I reply before I can stop myself, my voice rusty from disuse.

His mouth quirks up in a grin. "Oh, she speaks. Here, I thought you were a mute."

I narrow my eyes at him and give him my best condescending smile. Unfortunately, I'm quite out of practice.

He glances at the tray. "I wouldn't eat the meat if I were you, but the noodles aren't so bad." He nods and for the first time I notice the greenish glob of what could possibly pass as noodles made of seaweed on the tray. That is, if Xon 9 had surface water. I try not to gag. My face must turn a visible shade of green. "Like I said, you might want to try them. It would be an improvement from your regular rock-hard bread roll. Change it up a bit. Live a little."

I snort in reply. "Hard to live it up in a cell made of metal."

"Well, you never know." he says, shrugging. "I'll be back in a bit to collect the tray. *Bon appetite*, Princess."

I start at his words, but he's already turned his back to me as the door slides open and he steps back into the hallway. Princess. Only a handful of people have ever called me princess. Only two who knew what I really am. Who my mother really is. One is dead. The other is Li. My heart begins to pound in my chest as if it will burst out of the jail that is my ribcage. I look around my cell. There are no cameras in the cells. There are cameras in the hallway, but none in the cells. I inch closer to the tray. The smell makes my stomach retch. If not for the Imminent Darkness, the Leadership Council should be put to tribunal for making anyone eat this garbage, prisoner or not.

I swallow the urge to vomit and inch my fingers toward the tray. They don't give us utensils, just the tray and a small napkin. I pick up the roll and take a bite, practically cracking a tooth. As I chew I glare at the green glob. But he called me Princess. *Live a little. You never know.* I stop chewing and close my eyes. I take a deep breath. I can smell the staleness of the bread and the sea-like smell of the strange noodles. Wait. There it is. Just the hint of something metallic. That's the downside to taking away one of someone's senses, staring at metal walls all day, the other senses become heightened. Like superpowers. I don't need my Elemental gifts to confirm what my own nose has already told me.

I jab my fingers into the cold gloop. The noodles are slippery, but it only takes me a second to find it. A thin, silver pen-like object. No cameras. I pull it out of the glob. There's a small, black button that slides along the side. My fingers find the small engraved marking before my eyes do, the letter X and the number 9 along with three interlocking circles. The sun and twin moons. On the opposite side is another engraving: a tiny symbol like an upside down Y. This is a military grade laser cutter. That can cut through anything. Like a steel door. *Princess.*

Li.

What can I say? I know a guy.

CHAPTER 2

When Mr. Big Neck arrives to retrieve my tray, I watch him warily. My back is pressed against the far wall, sitting on the hard-as-concrete bed, my knees drawn up to my chest. He picks up the plastic tray that rests at the foot of the bed. I didn't eat the noodles, but their green gloop is slopped over the tray's multiple compartments. The roll rests nearby with only a single bite taken out of it. He glances at me with a raised eyebrow.

His hair is in a buzz cut and, unlike my friend Cerise who's red hair is kind of auburn, his is almost orange in color. His face is smattered with freckles and he's about as wide as the doorway. I can't imagine Li—all sinewy and hard lines—being friends with this guy. But then again, who isn't Li friends with? Or maybe he's friends with

Sloan, since they appear about the same age, and Li simply supplied the laser cutter. I wonder what his name is. If I'll ever be able to thank him.

My face reveals nothing, but my heart beats double time in my chest. Mr. Big Neck ducks back into the hallway, placing my tray on the wheeled cart before reappearing again with a freshly laundered jumpsuit. He places it at the foot of the bed, gives me a curt nod and disappears back out the door. I have exactly thirty seconds to change clothes. Showers are hard to come by in this place, I can count on one hand how many I've had since I've been here, but we can't have prisoners with dirty jumpsuits, now can we? When I was first locked up I had a cloaking cuff hidden on me, but it was quickly confiscated one fateful laundry day. I was given a freezing cold shower—the water stinging my head and shoulders—as penitence.

I deftly unbutton the column of buttons and shimmy out of the white jumpsuit, kicking it out of the way with my soft-soled shoes. My hair stands on end as the cool air pierces my skin. If they aren't going to starve me to death, then they may as well freeze me to death. I pick up the clean uniform, its metallic scent wafts over me. Even the laundry smells like Metal in this place. I jam my legs into the jumpsuit and quickly pull it up, but as I do I catch a glimpse of something along the seam. A tiny piece of paper. On just a passing glance, it would appear to be a clothing tag. Except it isn't. Whatever it is, it was haphazardly sewn into the jumpsuit's seam. A long white thread dangles from one side.

There's a brusque knock at the door.

"Ten seconds."

I yank at the thread and it begins to unravel, and as it does the tiny paper becomes free. I stuff it into my bra and finish buttoning the jumpsuit just as Mr. Big Neck comes back through the door. I take two steps back, still not trusting. It could be a trick. He could be the Imminent Darkness. The ID can take on almost any form, even the smallest of microbes. I've seen it with my own eyes. Energy cannot be created nor destroyed. It can only change form. I've been tricked before and as much as my heart wants this sliver of hope—a friend, a chance, anything—my head will not allow it.

Without a glance he picks up my dirty jumpsuit and gives me a slight bow before exiting back through the steel door. Before the door seals shut, he says: "Good night, Princess." To a passerby it would seem like a mockery, but to anyone who knows me—the real me—it's a whisper of truth, a beacon of light reaching out to me across the darkest of seas. To some it's a hope and to some it's a fear. But to me, it's the beginning of a battle cry.

. . .

I roll the soft paper between my fingers, heart pounding. It's so small. What words could it possibly hold? And yet the rush of life in my veins, the feeling as if I've woken from some sort of month long sleep has begun to fade away, and the edges of reality are coming into sharper focus. Sometimes we just have to wait.

The paper says: **MIDNIGHT ROUND** and that's it. Whoever wrote it—I assume Mr. Big Neck because the handwriting doesn't look familiar—was pressing very hard, the back of the small paper is lumpy with the lettering. Midnight round. I'd be kidding if I said I slept through the night. The guards do rounds every hour. I wrack my brain trying to remember the routine that I used to pay so much attention to, hoping for a chance to seize the moment. Only it never came.

At first, it was easy to keep track. The guards checked on me regularly, trying to determine if the new prisoner was going to give them any problems. I was docile enough though. I had known what had to be done. I knew what the statement of me being arrested would make to the others. Both to the ones who stand with me and the ones who stand against. The guards conducted hourly rounds, but eventually I lost track as the empty spaces seemed to expand and as the metal walls and anguished screams pushed in on me from all sides.

I knew I was in the maximum security wing. I had come here willingly, like a lamb led to slaughter, trusting in the ones that I left behind. I had to get answers and sometimes the only way to get answers is to creep in the den of monsters. I hadn't gotten any answers yet, but I had a feeling they would be coming, thanks to a heavy-footed, red-headed prison guard. I slip the paper back into my bra and curl myself into the fetal position on the hard bed. I absent-mindedly run my fingers along the Elemental Star tattoo on the back of my neck, feeling the bulge of the twisted green vines, and then the rough grain of tree bark, before moving to the smooth filigree of fire, and lastly to the single point of wetness, a wetness that does not spread and does not drip, but nonetheless is always present. Always present. Always there. Just like someone I know. And I know now is the night that I will finally find some answers.

. . .

I find myself in a strange room. A room that I've been in before. I know to my left is a winding stairwell that leads to the door leading out. To my right is an oblong window. The room is sparsely furnished: the wall adorned with tapestries—one for each of the five elements, an elaborately woven rug, a rocking chair, a small desk, and another plush velvet chair behind it. There's a light in the corner and it illuminates the leather-bound book which sits on the desk.

A shadow moves but I don't start. Even in the shadows, he's familiar to me. Sloan comes up behind me and wraps his arms around my waist encircling me, my back pressed against his chest. He sighs into my hair, which I know is greasy and reeking of metal. I turn in his arms and for the first time in I don't know how long, I look my boyfriend in the face. Because he is here. I am here. Sloan can read my thoughts and he can travel in my dreams, he doesn't have all of his mother's gifts, but a few. More importantly we are inextricably tied together because he is bound to me by his Everlasting Vow, a vow he took before he ever met me, to protect me and keep me safe. At the time it was because his mother had visions of the Impossible Girl and how she would somehow save the inhabitants of Xon 9, but now his vow is for a very different reason.

"I've missed you," he whispers. His eyes rove over my face and neck, searching for any signs of mistreatment, eyes glinting in the dim light. Before I have the chance to reply, he pulls me in closer and his lips find mine and he's kissing me as if I've been gone an eternity. He presses his hands into the small of my back, as if he could press me closer to him then we could somehow fuse into one person. I can feel the heat and longing in his touch. The lingering effects of our time in the Land of Water, but it doesn't make it any less real. I intertwine my fingers in his shaggy brown hair, in need of a cutting. His hands move up my sides until they stop at my rib cage and he pulls back unexpectedly.

"Kata." I can hear the chastisement in his voice. "You're half-starved."

I pull back self-consciously, suddenly very aware of what I must look like. Pale skin, sunken in eyes, greasy hair. All bones in a too big, prison-issued jumpsuit. I wrap my arms around my waist as if I could hide from him. I shrug. "I haven't been all that hungry."

He takes a step toward me. "I'm sorry. I was just—surprised. That's all. As soon as we get you out of there, Mrs. Chatfield will make you a proper meal."

"Why haven't you visited me?" I ask, leaning against the desk. My heart still pounding in my chest from the kiss. Just because it's a dream, doesn't make it any less real.

He sighs and runs a hand through his hair, sending it sticking every which way. "Believe me, I've tried. I've come here every night since you left. Every night I've come to this room and waited. Waited for you to come to me. But you never did. So, perhaps I should be asking you the same question."

He moves around the desk and pulls out the chair. I inch around the desk and sink into its soft plushness. Did the time pass just as slow for Sloan out here as it has for me in my cell?

"I—I tried. I mean. I couldn't sleep. Sometimes I could. But I never dreamed. Nothing. It's always nothing."

Sloan sits on the edge of the desk, his knee brushing against my elbow. He's wearing jeans and a button down shirt with the sleeves rolled up. I look up and when I really look at his face, I can see that his cheeks are slightly drawn and he has dark circles beneath his eyes. I never thought, that if Sloan visits me in a dream, does that mean that he is actually awake? I never asked how they did it, just knew that they could. Every night he came here, to this little tower in the middle of nowhere, and waited for me to come to him. He runs a finger along my cheek.

"I knew you would come eventually, once you had hope again. Once you were no longer afraid."

I laugh, but the sound is like a hollowed out shell. "Oh, I'm still afraid." I sigh, resting my forehead in my hands. "It was all for nothing. Just like everything else. I've learned nothing."

"Oh, but Ka, you've learned so much. You haven't been using your powers, but that's made the human parts of you that remain so much stronger. And now, we can put that to good use. You've met Bax, I assume?"

I reach into my bra and pull out the piece of paper. "Mr. Big Neck?"

Sloan chuckles. "I suppose he does have a rather large neck."

"Enormous," I correct. "Did you go to school together?"

He nods. "We grew up together. Both his mother and father were Unbalanced." Metal is the most easily Unbalanced of the Elements. "Now, we don't have much time. But did he give you the laser cutter?"

"Yes. It came from Li didn't it?"

"It did. You know, he always seems to know a guy. Even as the colony is crumbling around him, somehow that guy still knows where to go for the latest gadgets."

"Illegal gadgets." I absent-mindedly stroke the leather bound book that sits in front of me. "Midnight round. What happens then?"

Sloan crosses and then uncrosses his arms. He seems anxious. I probably should be too. "After you hear Bax pass your cell, wait until you hear him exit out the door at the end of the hallway. Wait two or three minutes, then use the laser cutter to remove the key pad. According to Bax, the key pad is approximately three inches to the door's right, which will be your left." He holds up two fingers to give me an estimate of the size. "The pad itself is about four inches square, so you'll need your cut to be slightly larger than that. Once you've cut through, use this to open your door." He reaches into his pocket and hands me a small piece of wax paper that's folded over.

I open it and there's a thin, slimy film between its layers. The film is mostly clear with a slightly blue tint to it. "That's an eye film replica. It's made in the likeness of Bax's exact eye dimensions. For how much we paid for it, it should work. Better work," he corrects. "Then after the door opens immediately use your Fire to disable the pad. That all should take you about ten minutes. After that, you'll have to hurry. Go down the hallway all the way toward the exit door, which should be marked. Then find Bax. He'll get you out."

"How will I find him?" I tuck the eye film next to the small piece of paper.

"With this." He reaches into his pocket and pulls out another item. But this one is familiar to me. It's a flesh colored ear piece that can be wedged into the ear canal for two way communications. "Li claims it's top of the line."

"Li thinks everything is top of the line." I take the small ear piece which doesn't even take up the entire pad of my index finger. I slip it into my ear. "How is he doing? Li."

"Considering his sister is recently deceased and his best friend turned herself in to a maximum security prison. I'd say overall, he handled it well. After Doran and I convinced him that he shouldn't go all vigilante and have his guy bomb the entire military complex, he focused more on a way to get you out. And, well, here we are." He grins. "Cerise may have helped a bit too."

I think back to when I first received my gift from Wood, the ability to witness the passage of time. I had seen Li, in the future, with a beautiful red-haired girl. He'd had a bow and arrow, which truth be told I'm not sure Li even knows how to use a bow and arrow, but the girl hadn't been one that I recognized. Until Sloan and I traveled to the Land of Water and I was rescued by a mermaid. A red-haired mermaid named Cerise, who was willing to sacrifice everything she ever knew for the chance to become human.

At one time, I had thought Li and I…but that seems so long ago now. I know Li almost as well as I know myself, all our secrets and our truths have been laid bare over the years. There's nothing left to explore between us.

I smile and it feels foreign on my face after so long. "I like her."

"Well, we know she's a badass with the dagger," Sloan's grin widens. He glances down at my finger that's still caressing the spine of the old, leather-bound book with its gold embossed lettering.

This book is my life. Or so Bina told me. It is my past, my present, and my future. I could know what the future holds. I could know if Li and Cerise end up together. If Sloan and I fall deeper in love and someday get married. With a turn of the page, I could know if and when I'll see my mother again. I slip my finger beneath the cover and run my finger along the smoothness of the inside. I could know if I beat the Imminent Darkness. If my home survives. If the people I love won't die.

"Kata…"

"This is how I saved your life, Sloan. Well, how Cerise and I saved your life. It was a page from this book. An incantation from my future. If I hadn't taken the page, I would never have known…" My words are swallowed up by an unexpected gulp of tears. The tears feel just as foreign as the smile.

Sloan pulls me out of the chair and up into his arms. I feel tiny and vulnerable in his embrace. All the time, ever since I found out who I was and what I was meant to do, I have felt stronger with each stone and more powerful. But now I am so tired. And I am scared.

Everyone I love—everyone that I have left—could die if I—we—can't stop the Imminent Darkness. I'm half-immortal. Everything I'd ever known would be gone. And I'd be alone. Sometimes I think it's the being alone that scares me the most. Because after being isolated from everyone for even such a short amount of time, I've felt what it can do to a person. Part of me has been forever altered.

"I don't really want to know," I whisper into his neck, breathing in his clean, watery scent, like he just came out of the shower.

"Once you know, you still can't change it. You can delay it, but it can never change." He strokes the back of my neck. His hands are warm and I press into him, suddenly needing to simply feel his humanness. Feel the solidity of his arms around me, his hand on my neck, and his breath on my cheek. "But it would change you."

"I'm already changed." And I am. I am a shadow of who I was before. The shadow of a girl who once seemed so familiar to me, but who seems like a fragment from a dream long ago.

"You are, Kata. But the beauty of life—whether mortal or immortal—is that you can always change again. You may not be able to go back, but you can always choose again."

Suddenly, the room feels like it's fading out of focus. Sloan's face blurs, then sharpens. His green eyes are surprised, but not alarmed. "I can't hold it any longer."

I nod. It's time to go. Time for me to wake up back in my prison cell and away from the comfort and familiarity of Sloan's arms. He cups my cheeks so that I'm looking him straight in the face, his beautiful, angular face. When he was my teacher—seems so long ago now—I had unknowingly studied every line and plane of that face, the arched bow of his lips, the shimmer of the scales that used to line his face. He kisses me and it's not a passionate kiss, but a fierce kiss filled with promises kept and an everlasting vow. The room spins, but this time it's not because the dream is ending.

When he pulls back his face blurs again, but this time it doesn't re-sharpen. The room begins to fade around us, growing smaller by the second. Disappearing as if being absorbed into the fabric of space time. "I'll see you soon. You can do this." I can feel him slipping away. I didn't realize how much I'd wanted—no, needed—him, to feel the physicality of him until it's being taken away.

His voice grows soft as if he's talking to me from the other end of a long tunnel.

"I love you," he tells me.

I can feel the hard wood of the bed beneath me and the sharp, metallic scent of my prison cell. In the space between sleep and wake, I realize that for the first time Sloan has told me that he loves me. But I didn't get the chance to say it back.

CHAPTER 3

There are no sounds except for the periodic scream that echoes down the hallway. My heart pounds against my ribcage. I feel different. Somehow I hadn't realized that I was letting them win. By allowing myself to be beaten down by the situation, it was as good as admitting defeat. And I hadn't even noticed it, until I was with Sloan again. Even if it was only in a dream, it was as good as real.

I feel the wax paper pressed against my skin. Sloan is my home. My mother and father are gone, living in another world, quite literally. But I belong here. Xon 9 is my home. The elements of this planet run through my veins as sure as anyone else's. Unlike everyone else though, they belong to me. I feel stronger than I have since I first entered this place. I run a finger along the inside of my wrist, outlining the tiny incisions. My Earth gift was a strange one. It is the ability to shoot vines from the inside of my wrists. If anyone tries to stop me—correction *Bax* and me—then I can bind them. I haven't used the power in a while, but I can still see the tinge of green in my veins even in the garish light of my cell.

All this time I'd felt alone. In reality, I was anything but alone. I sat here feeling bad for myself, while out there my friends were trying to find a way to help me escape. And hopefully they have because I can't imagine the cost if I get caught. I'm pretty sure by this point I've royally ticked off both the Imminent Darkness and the Council of Leaders, which just might be one and the same. The Council knew what was happening, and they did nothing to stop it. In fact, they could even be the reason for it. But I don't have all the facts. In typical fashion, I need more information, but I'm running out of time.

Ahna would know what to do. She always knew what to do. Smart and decisive. My stomach clenches at the thought of my best friend, thousands of tiny black insects incubating inside her until they destroyed her from the inside out. An insect bred from the Imminent Darkness. All it needed was one microorganism. As soon as it took that form and replicated, it could continue, no longer feeding off the ID's energy, but of its imprint. A swarm of insects that made it to the colony. That can crawl into eyes, ears, and mouths. That you might not notice entering into your body, and carrying with it a disease that will overwhelm your immune system and have you dead in days. If you're lucky. I know she would tell me not to say it, but in the end, I failed her. I may not have been able to save her, but I almost got her twin killed. And the memory of letting her down, the anger she felt toward me, will always be ingrained in my memory.

I close my eyes and listen. Far away, I can hear familiar, heavy steps just entering the hallway. Bax. My cell is closer to this end than its opposite. If you're listening—*really* listening—his steps sound different tonight. There's a slight spring right before each footfall. He walks with a heel to toe strike. But due to his size, Bax is lacking in any grace. His pace is also quicker than usual. I hear him pass my door. My body tenses and it's almost as though I can sense his need to pause, the hesitation, but he suppresses it and continues down the hallway.

My pounding heart has picked back up. After so long of doing nothing, it feels strange to have a plan. To have a reason. And then I have an idea. An idea that would make the last month more than worth it. But I'll have to convince Bax that it's a good idea. A smile blooms across my lips, still feeling foreign, but feeling more right than it ever has. I finally know how I can get answers.

. . .

After I hear the heavy door bang closed at the end of the hallway, I count to one-hundred-and-eighty in my head, to roughly wait the three minutes Sloan instructed me to wait. Then I slip the laser cutter out of my shoe where it was resting snugly against my instep. They don't turn the lights off in the cells, another reason time was so disoriented.

At the door I guesstimate three inches to the left from the frame.

I slide the button of the laser cutter forward and a green light appears. It will act as a guide to ensure my cuts are accurate. I push the button farther forward, and take a deep breath. A red light emits, slicing easily through the metal without a sound. It makes for fast work and I'm dragging the laser down and to the left, then up to make the third side of my square. As I move up, the key pad's tangle of wiring is exposed. I catch the square piece of metal in my free hand and place it gently on the floor.

I reach in and pull the keypad through the hole, leaving a small window into the hallway beyond. I slip the wax paper out of my bra and unfold it to reveal the eye film. The exact replica of Bax's eye looks back at me, and I can't help but feel creeped out. I don't want to get my fingerprints on the film, so I carefully hold it up to the retina scanner. The key pad comes to life and a small light at the top glows red as it silently scans the replica. I realize that I'm holding my breath, but I don't need to hold it for long as the red light quickly turns to green and the door to my cell slides open with a whisper of air.

The dimmer light of the hallway spills in forming a dark rectangle on the steel floor. I fold up the wax paper and place it back into my bra for safe-keeping, then get to work on destroying the keypad. Electronics make for the most incriminating witnesses. It's already been about six minutes probably, which means I need to hurry.

I wrap my fingers around the keypad's wires. The familiar feeling of needing to be scared rushes toward me from the dark recesses of my mind, but I'm not scared. I notice with a jolt, that I feel invigorated, the smile from earlier making an encore. I grin as I tighten my grip. In order to summon my Fire, I usually tap into feelings of anger, but this time I just think it—will it—into existence. I can feel the wires growing warm in my fist. They begin to glow, then little sparks jump up singing the sleeve of my jumpsuit. The machine begins to smoke and it lets out a low hiss. Its light flashes red then green, then back to red. It begins to blink rapidly until the changing color almost appears to be brown and then with what can best be described as a sigh, it dies.

I don't have much time now. It's only a matter of a minute or two before central security will realize that something's gone wrong, that a door opened that shouldn't be open. I hurry through the doorway, ignoring the impulse to turn and look back at the cell that I called home for the last month. That's one home that I won't be going back to. Rushing down the hallway, my steps are silent in my soft-soled shoes. The prisoners make no noise and a dimmed row of lights lines the wall near the ceiling. The floor is so clean and smooth and I'm careful not to slip as I make my way toward the big door at the end of the hallway. As soon as I reach it I have to find Bax. But he's not the only one that I need to find. I grin to myself, but it quickly fades as I realize with sudden panic that the door at the end of the hallway is opening.

And I'm smack dab in the middle of the hallway with a bunch of cell doors on one side and a windowless, doorless wall on the other. I have nowhere to go, nowhere to hide. I clench and unclench my fists ready to summon whatever power I may need. The laser cutter sits like a lead weight in the palm of my hand. I freeze as the door widens and a large figure steps into the shadows. My heart seizes then releases with a rush of relief. It's only Mr. Big Neck. I mean, Bax.

He stands in the doorway and gestures for me to hurry. I quickstep toward him, easily closing the space between us and he slides the door closed behind me. We're standing in a stairwell, dimly lit like the hallway, by bare bulbs that sporadically line the walls. Bax puts a finger up to his lips and I want to tell him, well no, shit, Sherlock. But I don't. I follow him as he begins down the steps.

The military complex is a strange building. It's not really a complex since it's one building, but it serves multiple purposes. Tribunals are held in Council Hall, but the military complex is home to many Metals. The top floors all consist of residences, including Sloan's sister Michaela's. The bottom floors are military offices: Arsenal, Stratagem and Tactics, Universal Intelligence, and so on. But the coup de grace, is the prison. It's located below the building and is spread several hundred meters wide. It's the only prison on Xon 9. For the most part—before the arrival of the Imminent Darkness— violations of the law weren't really an issue. Sure, there were minor infractions, and the occasional major one, but overall Xon 9 is a safe planet. Only, I'm learning that not everything is as hunky dory as the Leadership Council would have us believe.

We reach the next landing and located in the wall is a round door with a keypad next to it. Bax leans forward and it scans his retina before unlocking with a click. He uses the handle to pull the door open and it reveals a dark tunnel. From his waistband, he pulls a small flashlight and nudges me wordlessly toward the tunnel. I have to lift myself up to enter it and I'm weak from not eating much, my arms have gone noodle as they struggle with my body weight. Bax, who is a good six inches taller and fifty pounds heavier, reaches out and grabs the excess fabric of my uniform at the small of my back and unceremoniously lifts me and shoves me into the dark tunnel. He quickly comes in behind me and swings the door shut behind us with a final click.

He leans against the cool metal wall and lets out a long breath, which sounds as though he must have been holding it since he walked past my room.

"What took you so long?"

"I had to carve out and disable an entire key pad. It isn't like I was twiddling my thumbs," I snap.

Bax gives me a pained look. "I'm sorry, it's just that Li was scrambling the cameras and they're so high-tech he can only scramble them for a few minutes to allow us passage."

I know I should apologize, maybe even say thank you. After all, he's risking his job—possibly even his life—to bust me out of prison. Instead I ask, "Where are we?"

"Evac tunnel. In case of a riot or biohazard, guards can utilize the tunnels to navigate the entire building." He shines the flashlight down the tunnel, but all I can see is darkness. "The tunnels lead out to the ground level. Sloan will be waiting for us."

The mention of his name reminds me. "About that. There's something else I have to do before we leave."

Bax gives me a look as if I've completely lost my mind. Maybe I have. "Ka, I'm not sure you understand, but we are in the middle of a prison break here. There's no time to do anything else. Once they realize your cell is empty, this place will be teeming with guards." His tone isn't unkind, but matter of fact.

"If you can help me, I'll be out before then." I can see the hesitation in his blue eyes. I put my hand on his forearm. The only physical human contact I've had in a month, besides my dream. "Please. It will help Sloan," I add.

He sighs and looks down his nose at me. It looks as if that nose may have been broken a time or two. Was Bax always a prison guard? "Okay. What?" Loyalty lies deep with this one, and I would expect nothing less from someone who keeps Sloan's company.

"I want to rescue Finn too."

Bax closes his eyes and runs a hand through his buzz cut. "I'm not sure that's possible."

But I won't give up that easily. "We have to try. If you've been Sloan's friend for as long as he says you have—"

"When did you talk to Sloan?" he interrupts.

I feel my cheeks flush. "It doesn't matter. What matters is that you know Finn doesn't belong in here as much as I don't belong in here. His family needs him." Then selfishly I add, "And I think I need him too."

He's silent, as if weighing his options. I wonder if I'm just plain crazy for even suggesting it, but Finn has been tortured for speaking out against the Leadership Council and if anyone has information about them or the Imminent Darkness, it's him.

Bax opens his eyes. "This way. But hurry."

I smile gratefully. "Thank you."

And with no time to lose, Bax takes off down the long tunnel with me right on his heels.

CHAPTER 4

In whispered breath, magnified by the ear piece, Bax explains to me that the evac tunnels run throughout the entire building, not just the prison. There are no lights besides our flashlight and we periodically pass a round doorway like the one from which we entered. I'm panting as I try to keep up with him. A sharp pain has begun just beneath my rib cage. And I'm surprised I haven't rolled an ankle yet in these stupid, soft-soled shoes.

We turn left and right and back again, until I have zero sense of the direction that we're headed. We reach a metal ladder built into the wall. Bax climbs the ladder with ease, reaching the round door above and allowing the built-in keypad to scan his eye. The tunnels are sealed so that certain sections can be blocked off in case a pathogen is loosed, either by mistake or on purpose. I don't think now is the time to mention the swarm that headed toward the colony only a month ago, so I just bite my lip.

When the light glows green, he shoves it open and reaches down, yanking me up the last few rungs of the ladder and through the door before he swings it shut. Not only am I slow, but I've asked for Bax to break out not one, but two prisoners. And here he is doing it without complaint, but he isn't about to let my slowness be an additional liability. We continue down a new tunnel that looks just like all of the others.

"All these tunnels look exactly the same," I point out. The pain in my side is getting worse. Lack of activity and dehydration are working against me.

"I have a schematic," Bax replies over his shoulder. He hasn't let go of my hand since yanking me through the doorway, and now he's pulling me along as my feet try to catch up. The light from the flashlight bounces off the metal surrounding us.

"Where?"

For the first time Bax grins. He lets go of my hand and taps his temple with his index finger. "Up here."

"Wait." I pant. "You have a schematic in your brain?"

"I'm a solider. Certain soldiers have had certain…upgrades."

"As in bio-engineering. Cyberkinetics?"

"Something like that. Behind my left eye is a small chip that superimposes maps and schematics over my vision. So I pulled up the one for the tunnels and am following it down to the special ops ward. The technology is ingenious really."

"Special ops ward?" I ask as we round another corner.

"For prisoners who've been found guilty of treason or other crimes against the Council."

"There's an entire ward for that?" I'm speechless. Are there so many who disagree with the work and choices of the Leadership Council? Did I not hear of this because the dissenters were taken and locked up before anyone else could know?

Finally, Bax slows down and we stop. I try to catch my breath taking in small gulps of the mechanized oxygen that's pumped through the tunnels. To my chagrin, he's not even winded. He looks as calm as a Xon 9 breeze. And I sort of hate him for it. He's stopped by another round door with a keypad beside it.

"Hold on," he says and I watch as his gaze shifts, as if he's staring off into space. The pain in my side finally begins to subside and while I wait for Bax to do whatever it is Bax is doing, I try to think of the best plan to rescue Finn. He's blind, so it may slow us down. And old. That could also slow us down. Okay, not turning out to be the best win-win scenario of my life. But someone once told me that the hard things are the ones most worth doing.

"Okay, I think I have a plan," I say once my breath has returned to a somewhat normal cadence. "You can open the door and after it closes I'll disable the keypad. Then we run like hell."

"There will be cameras and Li doesn't know we're doing this so he can't scramble them."

"Fine. You return to the tunnel with Finn and I'll destroy them."

"How?"

"Don't worry about the how, just get Finn out of here and I'll be right behind you." He gives me a dubious look. He doesn't need to point out the sweat that still glistens on my brow for me to get his point. "Okay, *almost* right behind you."

"If you say so, Princess. Finn's cell is the third on the left. Should be a quick in and out." He makes toward the door, placing his right eye in front of the keypad.

"How do you know that?" I ask. One thing that I did learn during my time here is that certain guards are assigned to certain wards. This is the special ops ward, but I was kept in the maximum security ward.

Bax taps his temple again. The cyberkinetics. It must have some kind of tracking system for the guards. He leans forward and the keypad scans his eye, then the door opens with a resounding click. Show time.

. . .

We enter into the stairwell and I follow Bax down a flight of stairs. Suddenly, he shoves me against the wall and into the shadows. His back is to me and he's so close I can smell the laundry detergent of his uniform. I immediately scan the wall near the ceiling and notice a small black camera with a flashing green light. It doesn't rotate or sweep and is trained on the door leading into the special ops hallway. The hallway that we need to get into to rescue Finn.

"You'll have to destroy that one." Bax's voice floats into my ear. My chest pressed against his back, I hadn't even heard him speak. He's speaking in a barely audible whisper, but the ear piece picks it up perfectly. I'd nearly forgotten that I was even wearing it.

He continues. "I'll grab Finn. There's a camera in the hallway, but it's less suspicious if they only see me. It's not completely unheard of for a guard to be seen with a prisoner from another ward. You destroy the camera. If we're lucky, they'll just think it malfunctioned like the others."

"Destroy it. Got it."

"Then I'll bring Finn back this way and we'll head back into the evac tunnels."

Without another confirmation, Bax moves away taking with him the comforting reassurance of a partner in crime. He lets the keypad scan his eye. He pulls open the door and hesitates. I imagine him wishing me luck, but he says nothing and the door closes with a click behind him.

I stay to the shadows as I inch along the wall toward the camera. As usual, I haven't completely thought this through. The camera is high up and even if I stood precariously on the railing there's no way that I would be able to reach it. So, I close my eyes and think of my mother. My beautiful mother who more or less started this whole mess by falling in love. And I think of Ahna. The pair of them with the perfect curlicue of green vines along their neck, and wrapping behind their ears before climbing up the side of their faces. Intelligent, calm, and loving. With a jolt I feel a movement through my veins.

I push up my sleeves and the veins on the inside of my wrists seem to pulsate with life and I know what's coming next. Thin, green vines shoot out of the incisions on the inside of my wrists and I do my best to aim them at the camera. They follow my unspoken command and wrap themselves around the hinge of the camera, where it's attached to a pedestal that's attached it to the wall. And then I yank my wrists back, the camera dropping from the wall with a loud *crack!* As soon as I think it, the vines snap off and the ends retreat back inside my veins where they live in wait for my command.

I hurry over to the camera, its light is no longer flashing green, but yellow. Loud, heavy-footsteps echo from the behind the door, and I immediately recognize Bax's familiar step. I summon my Fire, no longer needing the fuel of my anger to create the tiny, delicate sparks. Part of me is fascinated by Fire. It's the Element that I pronounced after all, even if it was a colossal mistake. But I love it because it is everything that I think I am not. It's fierce and unpredictable. Volatile and passionate. It is the giver of life. The sparks dance out of my fingertips and fall onto the camera. It isn't long before it begins to smoke.

The door opens and I turn, still in a squat, ready to leap at whoever it is in case it isn't who I'm expecting. My heart is pounding. But it's only Bax, and with him is an older man with wild brown hair and milky, greenish eyes. He's hunched over as if he hasn't straightened up in a very long time.

"Finn." I breathe.

His chin darts up. "Ka?" His voice is rusty from disuse.

"This is a lovely reunion and all, but we need to go." Bax's eyes grow wide at the mess on the floor, which in my haste has truly created a lot of smoke. "The—"

But he's cut off by a sudden burst of rain. Only, it doesn't rain on Xon 9. And we're indoors. It's the fire sprinklers in the stairwell. An alarm begins to sound and the few lights turn from white to red, throwing everything in a sinister shade of scarlet.

Bax half drags Finn up the stairs, who stumbles as he tries to find purchase in these stupid, stupid soft-soled shoes. But even bare feet can leave identifying prints behind. I follow them taking the steps two at a time. By the time I reach the door to the evac tunnels, Bax is already shoving Finn inside. He grabs me and practically throws me into the tunnel. The door shuts behind him and he's off like a shot, darting past us and down the hallway, flashlight out and beam bouncing wildly.

I grab Finn's hand. "Come on!"

Our feet are soundless in the tunnel and even without the flashlight, I could easily follow the sound of Bax's heavy tread even in the dark.

"Where are we going? How did you get here?" Finn asks. He must have gotten a second wind because we're flat out running now and he doesn't even sound out of breath. Maybe he's prepared better for a prison outbreak than I have.

"Sloan. Li. Rescue." I pant.

"Who's Li?"

"A friend of ours."

We round a corner and reach another door. Bax scans his eye, opens the door, and begins to climb up the ladder. I direct Finn to the ladder and wrap his fingers around the rungs.

"Go on up. Bax is at the top."

He nods and begins to climb unsteadily up the ladder. I'm right on his heels. I can hear the alarm still sounding and it is eerie in the tunnels, bouncing off all its metal sides. I scramble up the ladder and through the doorway in the floor. Bax closes it behind us and before I can even stand upright he's off and running again. I think I might die before we even get to the outside.

I'm sprinting hard and in my Herculean effort I lose one of the stupid shoes, but I don't slow down. Bax is holding Finn's hand, leading him through the maze of tunnels.

"Not much farther." Bax calls over his shoulder.

And then I hear something. The slightest of clunks. As if someone…

"Bax," I hiss, knowing that my earpiece will still pick it up and transmit to Bax who is several yards ahead of me. "I think someone's in the tunnel."

"What? It's not possible."

Footsteps. Fast ones. Running down the tunnel. Scraping steps that aren't as graceful as they should be for someone who thinks she was born to be a soldier. My heart beats double time and I try to propel myself forward, pumping my arms as fast as I can.

"It is! Someone else is in here with us. I think—I think it's Michaela."

We reach the end of the tunnel, and Bax turns left into the next one.

"Just a little ways more."

I see the beam of the flashlight bouncing off the walls around me. I hear the click, but my brain doesn't put it together. And then the loudest sound I've heard in months reverberates through the tunnel. A shot in the darkness. I feel the searing pain spread over the back of my thigh before I realize that I've been shot.

"Bax!" I cry and stumble forward. And she's on me before I can even process what's happening. I hear the pounding of feet retreating away. At least Sloan will have Finn now. At least it wasn't all in vain.

I try to crawl away, but her arms are wrapped around my legs. I can smell the metallic scent of blood as it spills from me and onto her and onto the metal floor of the tunnel. My fingers can't find purchase.

"Oh, no you don't," she says and I feel the gun pressed into the back of my head.

"Is this really how it goes down, Michaela? You killing your brother's girlfriend?"

"My brother doesn't know what he's gotten himself into."

I turn so my cheek is pressed against the cool metal. "More like you're the one who doesn't know what she's gotten into." I gather up all my strength, fueled by adrenaline, and flip over sending Michaela sprawling, her gun and flashlight clattering to the floor. She scrambles to find her weapon and my eyes adjust to the darkness faster than hers do because I can see it and she's nowhere close. Fumbling blindly. I've been playing with the darkness a lot longer than she has. I take off my remaining shoe and slip out the laser cutter. I toss the shoe aside and silently I get to my feet.

I can see Michaela still scrambling on her hands and knees, feeling around for her gun. Her fingers are just about to reach it when I send vines flying toward her and they pull her down and onto her back, pinning her arms to her sides. Tighter and tighter as if they are going to smother the life right out of her. I snap them off and come to stand beside her. I pick up the gun and shove it into the waistband of my underpants because I don't exactly know what else to do with it.

I slide the button on the laser cutter and it immediately glows green. "Cut out the tongue of a traitor?" I ask her.

She glares at me and spits on the tunnel floor, her lips a snarl. "Then you'd be cutting your own, Freak." I immediately flashback to Universal History class. A girl with blonde hair—not Michaela— sitting in front of me, passing me in the hallways and calling me a freak, a weirdo, a nothing, knocking my books off my desk. Sloan helping me pick them back up. I cannot believe these two people share the same blood.

I hold the laser cutter near her jugular vein. It illuminates her face in a sickly green. "I heard you." I whisper. "I heard you standing outside my prison cell, pressing your forehead against the cold metal. I know what you were thinking."

She laughs, a scornful sound full of hate. "My mother and my brother may think you're something special. But I know you're nothing. You're just an Elemental flaw. There's not even a word for you. Tristen should have killed you when she had the chance. Moons know how many she had!"

I swallow down my reply. Michaela knew about Tristen? I realize with sudden satisfaction that my earpiece is probably picking up and transmitting this whole conversation to Bax, and to whoever else might be listening. I ignore her words and press on.

"You were wondering if you did the right thing, betraying what little family you had left. A family where you were already different. No special gifts. Then a girl comes along and she is all sorts of special, and your mother loves her and your brother loves her. And even your father. Jealousy is an ugly thing, Michaela. It can make us commit unspeakable acts."

I draw the laser cutter closer to her. Her face glows green. I see her blue eyes widen. Whenever I would see Michaela, her eyes would be full of hate for me and whatever she thought I was. But now they are full of something else: fear.

"But I'm not jealous of you, Michaela. In fact. I feel bad for you." I pocket the laser cutter, sending us back into complete blackness. "I don't want your blood on my hands," I whisper. "I've saved your mother, your brother, and even your father. Consider this me saving you."

And without a second glance, I run silently down the dark tunnel.

CHAPTER 5

"Bax?" I whisper as I reach a doorway. I have no way of knowing if this is the door out of the military complex.

"Princess? Bax here. Are you okay?"

"I'm fine. I've reached a doorway. Is it this one?" The sirens still howl in the distance behind me, soft echoes reverberating off the walls around me.

"Copy. Do you still have the eye film?" Bax's voice is clear in my ear and I wonder if he and Finn have reached the others. I can't hear anything in the background.

I reach into my bra and feel the wax paper. I unfold it in the darkness and hold up the eye film to the key pad. Its light changes from red to green and I re-pocket the folded up paper. The door is heavy, but I'm still moving on pure adrenaline. My heart continues to pound from my encounter with Michaela. Did the others hear it? Did they hear the things she said to me? That she knew Tristen was ordered to kill me? *When she no longer needs protecting, the world as we know it will end.* Bina's words drift back to me. As long as there are people in the world like Michaela and Tristen then I'll need protecting.

I step into the tunnel, the door thudding closed behind me. In this tunnel I can no longer hear the faint cries of the siren. My hair is damp from the sprinklers and falling out of its short ponytail, but I pad down the tunnel and realize immediately that this one is shorter than the rest and has a lower ceiling. If I reached up I could almost brush my fingertips against it. Bax would have had to duck the entire way. I reach the end rather quickly, but I don't see anywhere else to go. The tunnel just abruptly ends.

"Uh, Bax? A little help here?" I ask.

"Look up," Bax instructs. I do as he says, but this blackness is different. More encompassing and I can't see anything, so I stand on my tiptoes and reach up feeling along the ceiling. And then I feel it. The metal feels different here. Warm instead of cold. I feel around and the warm metal forms a circle just big enough for a person to fit through. A door hidden in plain sight, like so many of Xon 9's secrets. "That doorway leads to the next level. When you exit you'll be in another tunnel. This tunnel will lead you to the Chatfield Forest."

"Chatfield Forest?" I've never heard of a forest named that before. Then it dawns on me he's talking about the forest near the perimeter of the colony, the one that has an elaborate system of caverns and tunnels beneath it. The one where my friends are staying. Doran's mother, Chanice Chatfield, is a Metal who has always offered a safe place and protection to those affected by the Imminent Darkness. Now, people have fled as the Imminent Darkness's minions have grown stronger and more violent. Fled into hiding. Safe-keeping.

"I like it," I reply.

I don't feel a latch on the door and there's no keypad. As if reading my mind, Bax's voice appears in my ear. "It's like a sewer cover. You'll have to push into it and pop it open, then climb out and drop it back in place."

"I'm not as tall as you, Mr. Big Neck. How am I supposed to reach it?"

There's a muffled sound in my ear. "Mr. Big Neck? Is that what you call me behind my back?"

I grin in the darkness. "Nah. I just called you that to your face."

"Sticks and stones. I left something down there for you. When you weren't with us, just in case. An envelope on the floor. Listen, they need me in a tactical meeting. Things have changed since I've been seen and we've set off the alarm. Use what's in the envelope— it's from Sloan. Then make your way out the tunnel there's only one way to go. Once you're through, we need to close it off so no one else can come through. Time is of the essence."

"Envelope, Chatfield Forest, move my butt. Got it."

Bax goes silent and I feel around for the envelope. I find it easily enough and open it up, dumping its contents into my cupped palm. It feels like seeds. My heightened sense of smell tells me they smell like a combination of earth and sea. Zephyrus Seeds to summon the wind. But how will the wind get to me down here? I trust that Sloan knows what he's doing and I kiss my closed palm then throw the seeds up and toward the small opening.

At first nothing happens, the seeds just sprinkle back to the floor of the tunnel, but then I hear it. A soft, hissing sound that quickly crescendos into a roar. The seeds ping off the sides of the tunnel, and somehow none hit me. I imagine a tiny seed being whipped at you would be surprisingly painful. My ponytail whips at my cheeks and my loose uniform begins to billow around me. Then there's a forceful torrent of air pushing past me and up toward the ceiling, the force causes me to stumble forward. I catch myself before I fall, just as the wind pops the small door off the opening above my head and then before I can feel for purchase the wind is pushing me up toward it, lifting my feet off the ground, toes dancing in the air as I scramble at nothing.

This isn't the first time the wind has helped me out—as someone gifted with all the Elements, wind falls into the category of Earth— but it's still as exhilarating as the first time. I reach out for the ledges of the opening as the wind pushes at my bottom, like a friend giving me a boost, until I'm up and over the edge staring up at a dirt ceiling. The wind begins to die down swirling back into the metal tunnel below. And just as quickly as it started, it's gone.

I remember Bax's words and drop the heavy, metal lid back over the opening. This new tunnel is dimly lit by sparse torches of fire, just far enough apart that someone could hide in the shadows, but still enough to see by. I get to my feet, the red dirt is soft between my toes. To my left the tunnel ends and is nothing but a smooth, hard-packed dirt wall, so I follow the tunnel to my right, picking up speed as I go. I remember Bax's words that time was of the essence, so I begin to run. The pang in my side is long gone, the tendrils of adrenaline, Fire, and Earth still coursing through my veins.

There's a rumble above me and suddenly I realize what Bax meant when he said close off the tunnel. They're going to create a cave-in. I begin to run harder.

"Hey! I'm still in here!" I pant.

"I know. I know." Bax's voice has a slight tone of worry. "That's what I meant when I said time is of the essence. The detonator for the cave-in was set to a timer."

"You know—" I'm breathing hard and my legs feel like wet noodles as I sprint down the tunnel. In the distance I can see a soft glowing light. "You could have just said that. Instead of being all poetic."

"Sorry, but I can't help my true nature. Words are the canvas to my deepest thoughts."

"Gag." Rocks begin to tumble from above, hitting me in the head and in the shoulder. If I sprint any harder I think my heart may burst out of my chest and run ahead of me. I can feel the warm blood from my thigh wound trickling down my calf. Half-immortal, I keep telling myself. But it's the mortal part I need to be worried about.

"Make haste, Princess." More worry in Bax's deep voice.

"In English, if you please." I spit back, the glow growing brighter. A larger rock bounces off my shoulder and I wince. That's going to leave a mark. I throw my arms over my head for protection, no longer using them to propel myself forward.

"Ten seconds." And there's no hiding the panic. The rocky ceiling behind me begins to crumble in my wake. Big chunks hitting the dirt floor with a resounding thud.

"Geez, oh, Moons!" I cry.

"Did you say goons?" Bax asks trying to mask his panic. "Because I take offense to that."

But there's no time to answer. The falling rocks are catching up to me and I can see the end of the tunnel, opening onto a larger cavern. I've never been one for exercise, or any physical activity really, and if the Imminent Darkness doesn't kill me surely this will. I run as hard as I can toward the end of the tunnel. I can see the tent city just beyond and the outline of several figures at the end of the tunnel.

I recognize one immediately, as if I'm recognizing myself. His arms are outstretched. Waiting. I hurl myself across the last few yards of the tunnel and into his arms as a flurry of rocks comes crashing down behind me, sealing the tent city and Chatfield Forest off from the military complex. I knock Sloan backwards and onto the ground with the force of my leap. He lands on his back, arms still wrapped around me tight.

He runs his hands over my cheeks and kisses my dirt-covered lips, but I don't care. I am aware of others standing around us, but I see no one but him. His shaggy brown hair swept across his forehead. The dimple in his left cheek and the now smooth skin of his right cheek where his scales used to be, before the enchantment to save his life took them away from him forever. Intense green eyes, the deepest of emerald seas looking up at me with so much adoration. My light, my beacon, my protector. I am home and I can finally tell him the words I hadn't gotten the chance to say, the ones I was afraid I'd never be able to say to him.

"I love you too," I whisper against his shoulder and then all at once the adrenaline is simply gone and all that remains is the searing pain in my right thigh from his sister's bullet. "Oh, and I think I was shot," I add before everything goes black and I pass out in my Sloan's warm embrace.

CHAPTER 6

"Leave it to you to be so melodramatic," Li smirks. He's sitting in a canvas folding chair across from the cot that I'm stretched across. Cerise is bent over in a chair beside him, sharpening a long dagger with an opalescent blade, its handle made of a simple iron alloy. Her red hair is in a loose braid down her back and her cheeks are flushed. The two chairs are so close together that as Cerise sharpens her weapon, her elbow continuously bumps Li's knee but he doesn't seem to mind.

"It's not like I shot myself." I wince as I adjust myself to a seated position. Sloan immediately jumps up and takes my elbow, helping me ease myself up against some pillows. I didn't realize how badly I was wounded until the adrenaline had completely worn off.

After I passed out, I woke up lying here. My wound already

treated. Sloan explained that Mrs. Chatfield had pulled the bullet out, but I'd lost a lot of blood. Before I woke up, Chanice had left to discuss my return with Zechariah, the unspoken co-leader of the tent city. Zechariah is a bit older than Mrs. Chatfield, both Metals. Most of the people making up the tent city are Metal refugees from the Underground, but the last time I was here I'd seen every Element represented. It spoke volumes that other Elementals looked toward the Metals for leadership.

Metal is the strangest of all the Elements on Xon 9. Its physiological affect is extremely invasive and it's easy to become Unbalanced. A Balanced Metal is strong and strategic, making for the best soldiers. But an Unbalanced Metal can be dangerous. They're deceptive and cunning, almost to the point of seduction. Not to mention aggressive. That's why I thought the Underground was originally created. To keep the Metals apart from the rest of the colony. It wasn't until I met Bina, Finn, and the Chatfields that I realized it wasn't the rest of the colony that put them there, but more that they put themselves there. Of all the Elementals, Metals are the most misunderstood. Their secrets kept hidden in the red dirt of the Underground.

Sloan sits down by my feet, resting a hand on my shin.

"Hey, stranger!" A tall, mocha-skinned boy enters the tent. His hair is cropped close to his scalp and the silver filigree of Fire wraps up his neck, around his ear and continues up his cheek toward his right temple, glaringly bright against his dark skin. "I heard you were shot!"

"Word travels fast around here," I mumble.

Doran continues. "I also heard that it was Loverboy's sister that committed the grievous act." He plops down next to me, forcing me to wince and scoot over on the small cot that already holds too many people. Sweat drips across his brow and I surmise that he must have been training. Training for a battle where nobody knows what we're up against but me. And here I am sitting here, half-useless, my thigh throbbing with a dull ache.

"Yeah," Li chuckles over the scraping of Cerise's sharpening. "Not too bright trying to off someone who's half-immortal. No offense, Bro." Li says to Sloan.

Sloan scowls in response, but his eyes aren't angry. "None taken."

Technically, Li is immortal now too, due to the healing nectar he was given when he was attacked by the Imminent Darkness and almost died. The catch being he has no idea. Li's the type who would go and fling himself off the cliffs of the Mountains, just to see what would happen. Immortal doesn't mean that one cannot break every bone in one's body.

"Hey," I say, realization dawning. "That means that I should be able to heal faster. My mother told me that once. I'm useless sitting here twiddling my thumbs. I have a fifth stone to retrieve."

Sloan glances at me. "Metal."

"Metal," I agree. Each of the Lands has been drastically different, and I can't even begin to fathom what the Land of Metal will hold for me. Not to mention, now that the ID has infiltrated the

Elemental Abyss, I'm not sure how I'm even going to get to the portal. I cringe at the memory of the Unbalanced Waters whose bodies lined the shore of the Enchanted Lake, my friend Brooks among them. My fingers curl around the sheet that's draped across my body. If I could just get near the Imminent Darkness, I'd choke the evil right out of it.

"This Land of Metal," Cerise looks up from her sharpening and sheaths the dagger, continuing to twirl the sharpening stick like a baton. "What do we know about it?"

"Nothing," Sloan and I say at the same time.

"All I really know is that we used to be able to enter through the Elemental Abyss and that the Land was created for my Aunt Isa," I add.

"Let's hope she's more pleasant than your Aunt Tullia," Sloan mumbles.

He's absent-mindedly rubbing my shin back and forth, his fingers soft and sure. The Land of Water was not a pleasant experience for either one of us. My aunt tried to seduce Sloan, which would have cursed him, making him unable to return home and have to remain forever enslaved to Tullia. A watery prison. She even had the nerve to try and kill me with one of her monsters. Thanks to Cerise though, she didn't succeed. Still, it isn't on my list of top ten places to visit.

Cerise weaves the stick between her fingers. "We'll go with you."

"No!" I immediately object. "It's too dangerous."

"Really, Princess?" Li scoffs. "After all we've been through, at this point we *expect* it to be dangerous. It's when nothing goes wrong that we begin to worry. In fact, I'd be disappointed if it weren't dangerous." He grins impishly.

"If you're going, I'm going." Doran says. "It isn't fair that I didn't get to go on any of the other ones, except Fire. Unlike, Miss Half-Immortal, those cracked ribs from Tristen took forever to heal."

"But—" I object. But Doran's not having any of it.

"I started this with you, and I plan to finish it with you." His face darkens for a moment and I imagine he's remembering when he first chose to join me, shackled to the floor of the Fire Building's basement, long, scorched black marks forever emblazoned upon his back. I can't fix the past, but I can't take the future away from him either.

Sloan glances at me and gives me a defeated shrug. He's right. There's little sense in arguing with any of them. If I'm in up to my neck, they're at least in up to their waists. The Imminent Darkness affects us all and the more help I have the better.

"Well, how are we going to get there?" I ask.

"Get where?" A rough voice comes from the tent's entrance. I shift uncomfortably to get a better look.

The man is tall, with slightly rounded shoulders. He's lean and fit looking, his brown hair cropped short. Metallic threads line the side of his face and his skin is wrinkled, but mostly around the eyes. Which are a milky greenish-white.

"Finn?" I ask at the same time that Sloan says, "Dad."

He has a long, thin stick and he uses it to guide himself into the tent. Doran finds an empty chair and guides Finn toward it. He sits. I don't know what kind of reunion Sloan and Finn had while I was passed out. Sloan's relationship with his dad is a delicate one. But he does clean up pretty nice and I can see traces of Sloan in his features. In the curve of his cheekbone and set of his jaw.

When Sloan was young, his father worked for Universal Intelligence. During his research, he found evidence of the Imminent Darkness and accused the Leadership Council of hiding information about it from the colony. Needless to say the Council didn't take kindly to the accusation. They tortured and imprisoned Finn, blinding him—literally—from being able to see the truth. I don't know much, but I know that Sloan was very close to his father before he was imprisoned and that the family dynamic certainly changed after he was gone. I don't know how many times Sloan visited him over the years, but I think it was few because it was simply too painful.

Now, that he's sitting here in this tent with us, it's hard to believe that my risk paid off. Sure, Bax probably can't ever go back to being a prison guard—not that he'd be able to once they discover he'd helped the Impossible Girl escape—and, yeah, Michaela shot me. But Finn is safe now. And more importantly, he's free. Well, as free as it gets these days. No one is truly free until the Imminent Darkness is gone for good.

"You didn't answer my question. Get where?" He rests his hands on top of his cane. Sitting here across from us, he looks like a different man. Not only is he cleaned up, but he's wearing a black t-shirt and jeans with boots. An elaborate tattoo of a phoenix winds up his forearm, its tail encircling a blazing sun down near his wrist.

When he moves his forearm the bird almost appears to be flying. I know the symbolism of a phoenix. A phoenix is an Ancient Earth Mythology bird that would die in a burst of fire and be reborn from its ashes. I wonder if that's how Finn is feeling right now: Reborn. He certainly looks it.

"Back to the Elemental Abyss," Sloan explains. "The Imminent Darkness has used it to travel to the different Lands. It killed all the creatures in the lake."

Finn's chin shoots up. "All of them? Are you sure?"

"It would appear that way. The lake was poisoned with its dark energy. The creatures crawled out of the lake, choosing to die that way instead." My voice is steely. I can still remember Brooks. His beautiful green eyes and black hair, despite the scales that ran over the majority of his face. The playful way he called me Princess before anyone else did. It isn't fair. But I learned early on the Imminent Darkness isn't about fair.

"Do you have a memory object?" Finn asks.

I glance at Sloan and he shrugs. He doesn't know the same things that his father does.

"Only my ring. And it only brings my father to me. My mother took the key…and that's it."

Finn is quiet for a moment, his brow furrowed. "I might be able to make one."

"But that's magic, isn't it?" Sloan objects.

"And so is the Imminent Darkness. Magic is simply a different use of energy. It's no different than the Imminent Darkness being able to transmutate. Magic is just conducted at the cellular level," Finn explains. Now I know why Sloan wanted to be a teacher.

"You take all of the fun out of it when you explain it like that," Li mumbles.

"So wait. Don't Sloan and Bina do magic all the time?" I ask. "The mind reading thing and the dream walking…that's all just magic isn't it?" Sloan tilts his head, curious. Unsure.

"Wait," Cerise says pointing the sharpening stick at Sloan. "You can read her mind? That's not very fair all things considered."

"Don't worry, she has powers all her own. We're pretty evenly matched," Sloan reassures her.

And it's true. Not only can I see a time lapse of someone's life, but my Water allows me to tell when someone is lying, with a slight shimmer of their facial features. It's not my favorite of the gifts because when you think about it, sometimes we're better off not knowing the whole truth. It was a surprising gift coming from Tullia, but maybe that's why she gave it to me. Her whole life seems to be a lie. I push the thought of my wretched aunt aside.

Finn turns toward my general direction. "To answer your question, Ka. It's not quite the same. The gifts Sloan and Bina have are much like yours, it's genetics. Whereas, true magic is a manipulation of energy at the cellular level. In this case, in order to create an object with a living memory, I'd be conducting magic at the sub-atomic level."

"You lost me somewhere between the words cellular and sub-atomic," Li says. His warm eyes meet mine across the tent and I see the flash of pain in them, and I instantly know we're both thinking the same thing. Ahna would understand. This would be right up her alley. She would have been able to learn so much from Finn. Maybe he would have even been able to learn some things from her too.

"Don't you worry about the *ifs* and *hows*, you all just worry about the when. I'll take care of the rest. When will you be leaving?"

"As soon as possible," I say as Sloan answers, "Not until Ka is one-hundred-percent."

"Okay, seriously. You two need to stop doing that. It's really creepy." Cerise stops twirling the stick and gives an exaggerated shiver. Li takes the opportunity to drop an arm across her shoulders.

"No worries, Babe. I'll keep you warm." Cerise rolls her eyes, but doesn't push his arm away.

"I agree with my son on this one, Ka. You're no good traveling to the Land of Metal injured. Yes, you're half-immortal, and you should heal quickly. Maybe in about two days' time you should be almost a hundred percent." He rises shakily to his feet. "Which means I have some work to do." His face moves around the tent, eyes unseeing, head tilted slightly as if he's listening for something. "Where is that big buffoon?"

"You mean Bax?" Doran asks.

"That's exactly the buffoon I'm referring to. He's supposed to be helping me, but he disappears more than he appears."

"Maybe he's magic," Li snorts under his breath. Cerise smacks him on the shoulder and I suppress a smile.

"Come on," Doran says guiding Finn's elbow toward the tent's entrance. "I'll help you find him. He's probably training. Those big buffoon types like to grunt and hit things. A lot."

Finn chuckles as he follows Doran out of the tent.

Sloan immediately turns to me, concern washed over his face. "Will two days be long enough?"

"It should be. I just need to get my strength up. I think I'm more mentally exhausted than anything." I finger the sheet.

"You know, I think I need some target practice," Cerise announces a little too loudly. She stands up and yanks Li up with her.

"But I want to—" Li objects.

"No. You don't," Cerise corrects. "And if you keep it up, you're going to be my target." She pulls him toward the tent entrance.

"Yes, ma'am!" Li salutes her with his free hand then gives me a wicked smile over his shoulder.

The silence of the tent feels heavy and I lean back and close my eyes. Sloan moves from by my feet to the outer side of the cot, gently helping me move over. I turn into him, taking in his clean, soapy scent. I notice he no longer has the lingering, salty smell of water. Li's Fire had burned up inside him during my battle with the army of Fire, but where did Sloan's Water go? Did it simply evaporate?

He puts his arm around me, resting his chin on the top of my head. My ear is pressed to his chest and I can hear the steady rhythm of his heartbeat, like a soft drum that anchors me to what I have left, the one thing that I haven't yet lost. That I will not lose. *When she no longer needs protecting, the world as we know it will end.*

"I'm sorry for everything that's happened." Sloan finally speaks, his voice is soft and sleepy sounding. How many sleepless nights did he have, trying to visit me in my dreams while I was gone, but never finding me?

"It was my choice."

"I know. But it didn't have to be. It seems futile. We learned nothing, except that my sister is a murderer."

"She didn't succeed," I point out.

He gives a half-hearted laugh. "If you didn't have your powers, she most likely would have."

"We rescued Finn."

He gives the top of my head a kiss. At some point, I'd been cleaned and bathed. My hair no longer a greasy mess. "And I'll forever be in your debt for it."

"It doesn't work like that," I mumble against his chest, my eyelids growing heavy as the sudden rush of sleep barrels toward me.

"What doesn't?" he asks. His cheek is nestled against my head.

"This. Us. No tallies are being kept." For the first time in a long time, I finally feel safe, here in Sloan's arms. A tiny voice inside my head says, *Yes, but for how long?* Because I am half-immortal and Sloan is not. What will happen when he grows old and is no longer there to keep me safe? What happens when I continue on living and the person I love the most doesn't? I'll be alone. Utterly alone. I felt that once, in a stark prison cell hundreds of meters beneath the ground. I know the thoughts that can poison a person's mind when they're alone for too long with nothing else to do but think.

And I never want to experience that again.

CHAPTER 7

I find myself back in the strange tower. Everything looks the same except Sloan isn't here. I run my fingers along the edge of the old, wooden desk. A breeze drifts through the window and brings with it some kind of floral scent. Jasmine? Gardenia? Whatever it is, it reminds me of my mother. Stepping toward the velvet chair, I notice immediately that in this place—dream or reality, it's sometimes hard to say—I am healed, at least for the time being. Yet, I'm wearing the same t-shirt and loose fitting pajama bottoms that I had on earlier.

I'm barefoot and the woven rug, with its elaborate, colorful design is soft beneath my feet. The book sits where I left it last, brown leather staring up at me. A book of my life, or so Bina had said. Why would someone leave this book here?

It seems dangerous to try and know the future. I mean, look at

Bina. The Sight hasn't exactly been kind to her. It's aged her more than her years and put her life in jeopardy. What happens when you see something that you'd rather not? Would Sloan still have taken an Everlasting Vow if Bina had never seen my face? Would I even be here if Bina hadn't seen it? My skin prickles. What if the only reason I am here at all is because Bina saw it and thought it would be so? Maybe we're all just figments of one another's imaginations. My head begins to spin with the weightiness of all these thoughts, coalescing and bumping against one another in the confines of my brain.

This book saved Sloan's life. I touch the cover gently, as if it is an old friend, but a friend who you know could turn on you at any moment. I glance up at the rocking chair, half-expecting to see Sloan or Bina—or even my mother—sitting there. But I remain alone. I pick up the book, it's heavy in my arms, and pad over to the empty rocking chair. There's an afghan draped over the back of it and I wrap it around myself, placing the book in my lap.

From this angle, I can see the sky out the window. It is not the sky of Xon 9. Not the sky of my home. Although lately, I've been wondering just where home is for someone like me. This is a nighttime sky, inky blue-black, like a bruised plum. Unlike at home due to the never-setting sun, here I can see millions of tiny pinpricks of white light. I close my eyes and just inhale the strange, but familiar floral scent.

These dreams never let me leave until its purpose has been served. And since no one seems to be making a guest appearance, I'm in no hurry. I feel safe here, and it seems there are so few places that I feel that way these days. I'm not sure what it means that the only place I feel safe is inside my own head. It seems to make both perfect sense and yet is counterintuitive to the peculiar sense of loneliness that now seems to drag behind me like a shackle.

I hold the future of my life in my hands, but instead of looking at the future, I decide that I'd rather look at the past. I turn the first few pages, skipping over what appears to be the table of contents. No spoilers here. Not if I can help it. I flip a few more pages and find the first chapter. It's a familiar story. The one where my mother met my father and fell in love. I'm not sure there's anything much more tragic than a mortal and immortal falling in love. I feel a pang of guilt again at Li. He will outlive Cerise. He will outlive us all. But he will have to move on as the world and people around him grow and die, he will endure. It is not something I would wish on my own worst enemy. Selfishly, it saved him for this lifetime. The lifetime he has with me. My stomach lurches with guilt. I will have to tell him eventually.

The next page is about my youth and when my aunts gifted the stones to my mother upon my birth. The same stones later given to Bina for safekeeping. Maybe Bina—with a unique magic all her own—was drawn to my mother like a moth to a flame. Like attracts like, after all.

A few pages later it's the story of when my mother first realized just what those gifts were and summoned Bina to help find a way to protect me. Mother had to throw each of the stones into the Elemental Abyss with the words *protection, piety,* and *promise.* It would protect me, but only for so long. Until I had to choose.

Then all would go to hell in a hand basket, I think. I flip ahead to my Pronouncement. It feels long ago, but was only several months. I can still feel the sweatiness of my palms as I stared at the engraved, silver buttons each representing an Element. And I can still hear the voice of the box recommending me for Water. We still get to choose. You can ignore the recommendation and follow your heart's desire. But it doesn't always mean it's the right choice.

I continue skipping ahead. The book chronicles my trips to the various Elemental Lands. My retrieval of each stone and its subsequent destruction. If I'm being honest with myself—which is something I've been working on lately—Metal scares me the most. I thought it would be Water. And trust me, Water was downright frightening, what with ancient sea creatures and my vain, egotistical aunt and her curses that turned human men into mermen bound to her forever and used for her amusement. But Metal is something different. It's not like the other Elements.

My fingers stop at a chapter called *The Secret of Metal.* I freeze, running my finger back and forth over the words as if I could erase it. Metal is strong and unbreakable. When in Balance, a Metal is the most devoted and talented of soldiers. When Unbalanced, they are conniving and dangerous both to themselves and those around them. And yet, they are probably the most misunderstood of all the Elements. I think of my friends now. The majority of them are Metals: Bina, Doran, Zora, Mrs. Chatfield, Zechariah, Finn, and Bax. Unyielding in their loyalty and true in their friendship. Willing to risk their lives in a blink of an eye for the greater good, for the ones they love and care about. Why is it then, that they are the most feared of all the Elements? Why is it that my parents warned me against going to the Underground and the Black Bazaar?

I could find out. My fingers smooth out the page in the book. The paper is thin because the book is so large, fragile like the wings of a dragonfly. All I would have to do is continue reading. I could find out why their bodies are so sensitive to the physiological change the Metal induces inside of them, why they isolate themselves from the other Elements. Is it something as simple as the rest of the colonists fearing that which is different? Fearing that which they do not understand.

My heartbeat quickens slightly. I hear the distant roll of thunder outside the window. I glance up. There's a golden haze wrapped around the full moon. I can hear the gentle pat of rain drops hitting the stone window ledge. Lightning cracks across the night sky, illuminating the small room in a frightening blue glow for a second before disappearing just as quickly as it appeared. I close the book and press it to my chest. The warning seems ominous. The rain begins to fall harder until it sounds like fingers *tap-tap-tapping* over and over again on the outside of the stone tower.

I know Metal has their secrets. But they are secrets that will continue to be revealed to me slowly, like the gentle pulling back of so many rose petals, revealing layer after layer of velvety skin. With the afghan still around me I get up and walk over to the desk, placing the book back where I found it. Some things remain best unknown. I pull the desk chair to the window, which has no glass panes and is wide open. Cool drops of rain occasionally spatter against my face and I wrap the afghan more tightly around my shoulders. I sit down and rest my cheek against the tower's cool stone window sill. Secrets find their strength in the not-knowing. Once a secret is known, it no longer can hold its power. I close my eyes, the sound of the rain hypnotizing me toward sleep. Secrets *are* power. Maybe that is the secret of Metal.

. . .

Two days' time goes by faster than you would think. Sweat drips down my cheek as Li puts me through defense tactic after defense tactic. Right now he has his knee pressed into my back and my sweat-covered cheek is being squished into the blue training mat.

"Careful with my girlfriend! I like her in one piece!" Sloan grins as he and Cerise throw daggers into a wooden target on the opposite wall.

"Well, just think what you could do with two!" Li grins back. But he obliges and lifts his knee off my back. I roll over so that I'm on my back looking up.

My hair is sweaty and sticking to my forehead and neck. It's hard to believe only two days ago I was lying on a cot unconscious with a bullet wound. Sloan took the bullet Mrs. Chatfield had extracted from my thigh and had Doran create a necklace out of it. Doran is quite the jewelry maker, he even made my turquoise ring—which Sloan had held onto for safekeeping—that allows me to contact my father. But for this particular necklace he just drilled a hole into the bullet and thread a leather cord through it. However, if you look very closely you can see tiny engraved letters: *SB+KW.* Sloan Braden and Ka Waylon. The necklace is tucked beneath my sweat-drenched t-shirt.

Li extends a hand to help me back up to my feet.

"Come on now, Princess. You look like you've been to the land of the dead and back again." I clasp his hand and he yanks me up.

Given the circumstances, I think I'm doing pretty well. Mrs. Chatfield has been feeding me a steady dose of herbal concoctions. I'm still thin, but I feel stronger.

"I don't know why I need to train when I have special powers," I grumble. I took a hit to the cheek earlier and I can already feel a bruise blooming. So this is what they've been doing? Weaponry and physical training. It may work on the ID's minions that are causing mayhem around the colony, but they haven't seen the Imminent Darkness. No dagger, bow and arrow, or even gun can kill that thing.

"Ah," says a familiar voice. "But what if you don't have your powers?"

I whirl around to face Bax, whose neck somehow looks bigger than ever if that's even possible. He looks in pristine condition, except instead of a prison guard uniform, he's wearing fatigues and a black tank top, and he has muscles on top of his muscles. A tattoo of two moons flanking a sun above the horizon of a red planet covers one bicep. On his other bicep is a portrait of a woman with the word *remember* scrolled beneath it. I wonder who she was and what happened to her. I try not to stare.

"And just where would my powers go?" I ask hotly.

"Nothing lasts forever, Your Highness." Li slings an amicable arm around me and I immediately use his own tactic on him, quickly shifting my body weight beneath him and using my hip to flip him up and over my shoulder. He slams into the mat and grimaces.

"Good. You're learning," he groans as he rolls to one side.

"What do you mean?" I rub the insides of my wrists. "They're not going anywhere."

"Possibly," Bax shrugs. "But using them would be a dead giveaway of who you are. At times there may be the need for discretion. And that's why you're practicing hand to hand combat." He looks down at Li who's still groaning on the floor like a big baby. He can throw me around and be smug about it, but as soon as he gets a taste of his own medicine it's all *woe is me*.

Bax continues. "That was good, but what about someone bigger?"

I shift uneasily. Li is one thing. I've known him practically my whole life. I know his body and his movements. I can take advantage of his weaknesses and exploit my strengths. But someone like Bax is a different beast all together. Literally. I see Sloan glance over his shoulder, his eyes uneasy.

But he has a point. If we have to defend ourselves, it may not be wise to give myself away. I have to be able to protect myself and the ones that I care about.

"Okay," I agree hesitantly. "But keep in mind I can't be laid up for another couple of days. Tomorrow, I need to travel to the Elemental Abyss. I've already wasted too much time."

"Yeah, yeah. Princess. I get it. Don't break the merchandise." He jerks his head toward where Sloan has frozen, holding a dagger poised to throw, but too intent on listening to the conversation behind him. "I wouldn't do that to Sloan anyways. I just saved you. I'm not about to break your ribs."

"How comforting," I mumble. Li seems to have recovered and gets to his feet, stepping off the mat and standing to the side to watch, arms crossed.

Bax tilts his chin from side to side and there's a series of cracks and pops. I gulp. If he's not trying to break me, he's not doing a very good job of being convincing. His pale eyes fall on mine.

"Lesson one. Psychology. All I did was crack my neck and I can already see that your pupils are dilated. When we're afraid, our pupils dilate to allow in more light." I close my eyes and take a deep breath. Then open them again. "Better. Now. Lesson two. Body mechanics." He comes over and grabs my arm. I immediately go rigid. He swiftly kicks my feet from beneath me and I land on my butt. I'm thankful for the cushioned mat because that would have definitely left a mark. He immediately helps me to my feet.

"Now, make your body loose. Relax. Think languid water. Just flow." And before he finishes the word *flow*, he's knocked my feet out from under me again. But this time I keep his instructions in mind and keep my body as loose as possible, like limp rope and it's easy for me to break out of the fall and roll back onto my feet and into a crouched position. There's no hesitation. It's an automatic instinct.

Li nods approvingly and Bax smiles. "Good. You learn quickly,

Princess."

By now Sloan and Cerise have stopped throwing daggers and have joined Li on the side of the mat. Sloan's face reveals no emotion, but I know that he trusts Bax. If he didn't he wouldn't have asked him to help me break out of prison. And Bax wouldn't have risked losing his job in order to do it.

"Last lesson."

"Only three?"

Bax shrugs. "I like to keep things simple." Suddenly, his arm shoots out and his fist is heading right toward my right cheek, the one without the bruise. Except it stops right before impact, his knuckles grazing my cheek. I freeze, unable to imagine the amount of strength it must take to reign in a punch that's already been set in motion. Just what kind of training do they give to these soldiers? "Always watch your opponent's eyes. It might be subtle. But the body follows where the head and eyes go. It's like if you're balancing on one foot. You can do it just fine with your eyes open, but close them and your body begins to sway and you fall over. Often times, our eyes look at the target before we're even aware that it's happening. Try again."

I let out the breath I'd been holding, the one that would have braced me for the impact of the punch that never came.

He dances around me a bit, to the left then to the right. Waiting for me to expect it. And I wouldn't have, if I didn't follow lesson three and see his pale eyes almost imperceptibly dart to my waist. I block the punch with my forearm just before it can hit my gut.

Bax smiles. "Very good."

"You did that on purpose though," I said. "You're a trained solider. Your eyes wouldn't betray your intentions."

His grin widens. "True. But most people aren't trained like we are. So it will be to your advantage." He bites his lip as if thinking then says, "Let's try one more thing."

I shrug. *Why not?* I'm still in one piece so far. I took more of a beating from Li than I am from Bax. *Hopefully, not speaking too soon*, I think.

"Close your eyes," Bax instructs.

"Wait. What?"

"You've got to be kidding me," Li says from the side. "I know you're friendly and all mate, but isn't that a bit of an unfair advantage?"

"Shush," Cerise scolds. "Let the man teach." Li rolls his eyes, but obliges. Sloan shifts from foot to foot, obviously uncomfortable, but not wanting to contradict whatever lesson his friend is about to impart on me.

"Fine." I close my eyes.

"Now, just listen."

"That's it?" I ask opening an eye. He nods. And I close my eyes again.

At first I can't hear anything over the anticipatory thudding of my heart. My brain knowing that a punch, a sweep, or a kick is imminent. But I try to slow my breathing down, allowing my stomach to inflate on the inhale and deflate on the exhale. The beat of my heart slows and I can hear voices in the distance. People talking amongst the rows of tents. I tilt my head, trying to focus. I hear Cerise whisper something in Li's ear, and his soft laughter in response. I hear the quiet click of Sloan's jaw as he anxiously awaits Bax's next move. And then I hear it. The almost imperceptible sound of Bax's boots against the mat, the familiar heavy-stepped tread. Then the rush of air against my cheek.

Without opening my eyes, I throw up my right hand and my open palm intercepts Bax's punch. I open my eyes, and then turn using his own momentum to shove him past me. Surprised, he stumbles forward and catches himself. But when he turns back around I realize I'm wrong. It's not an expression of surprise that Bax's wearing, but of satisfaction.

He stands up and swings a big hand to pat me on the back, like a proud father. "That's what I thought."

"What did you thought?" Li asks staring at me with wide eyes. Cerise and Sloan's expressions mimic his.

"That while your Impossible Girl was locked away, she honed the ability to use her other senses. She doesn't need any special Elemental powers now because she's got her own. And she doesn't need any magic stones to access them."

I grin, wishing that were only true. Retrieve the five stones. Destroy them. Restore what's rightfully mine. Then rid my home of the Imminent Darkness. Forever. But I have the feeling that I'm going to need more than heightened senses for that last one.

CHAPTER 8

After a shower, Sloan heads with me to find Finn. Earlier Doran had said something about a workshop, and now the two of us are navigating the rows of the tent city. While I was gone, Sloan stayed here with Mrs. Chatfield. Bina, as far as we know, is still staying with Michaela. Despite how crazy Michaela may seem, she'd never hurt Bina. In fact her hatred for me stems directly from her love for her mother.

We pass row after row of tents. It's a simple set up really. As the Imminent Darkness minions grew stronger, the colonists fled. Chatfield Forest is between the perimeter and the Mountains of Xon 9. Our colony is small, only about 3,000 people. We never expanded much past the original settlement, and nobody seems to know why. I have a sneaking suspicion the Imminent Darkness is in cahoots with the Leadership Council, but I've yet to prove my theory true. Although, lately it isn't looking very promising for the Council.

The tent city has expanded since I was last here. More people fleeing and seeking sanctuary. Mandatory curfews, the closed University Complex, and increasing incidents of theft and violence—something that used to happen so rarely among the colonists—has stirred up fear. *Power is the reward. Fear is the currency.* Some people are talking in hushed whispers, a few—mainly Metals—have continued their work, selling and trading their various wares: jewelry, trinkets, food and drink that you could only find in the Black Bazaar. We pass a bored looking girl with her hair in elaborate braids on top of her head, ingrained lines like bark on the side of her face, spinning some clay on a pottery wheel. I guess you have to do something to pass the time. I may feel like I'm walking an impossible path, but it doesn't mean the rest of the planet stops spinning because of it.

Sloan stops and I almost run into him, lost in thought. To our right is a small, carved out cavern. There are several long, wooden tables with tall chairs probably built from the wood of the surrounding forest. Last time I was here, I'd witnessed a tactical meeting in a different cavern. It would appear that this system of underground caverns and tunnels is fairly adequate for a makeshift city. I wonder how long these tunnels have been here.

Around the work tables are a few people, Finn among them and Doran by his side. Finn's firm voice drifts over and I can tell that he's given Doran some sort of instructions. Doran is holding a clear cup and as we walk over I see that it has some kind of molten metal inside it. The substance is somewhere between a thick liquid and a moving solid. As Doran tips the cup to one side the silver substance creeps up the side and then slowly back down again.

"What's that?" I ask pulling one of the tall chairs over to the table.

"It would appear," Doran says looking up at me with confident, brown eyes. "that this is some sort of magical concoction that can transform any object into a memory holding one."

"Dad, you never mentioned you were an alchemist," Sloan says, plucking the glass from Doran's hand and inspecting its contents. He smells it and makes a face

"You don't know everything about your dear, old Dad," Finn smiles. He's missing a couple of teeth but the smile is no less cunning.

He turns to me. "Now, do you have an idea for an object?"

I lift the bullet necklace from over my head and place it into Finn's hand, wrapping his fingers around it. "How about this?"

His fingers feel along the cone-shaped bullet and rub the long leather cord that's knotted on one side. "I never did apologize for my daughter's actions. I thought that we'd raised her better—no, not better—*differently* than that."

"I'm used to it," I reply without thinking. Finn raises an eyebrow and Doran laughs. "Besides when we first met, Michaela has never liked me very much. She feels that I'm a threat to your family."

Finn considers this, still holding the necklace. Sloan rubs a hand back and forth over the smooth top of the table, waiting for his father's response. "And are you? A threat that is?"

"Only to someone who doesn't want anything to change."

"Ah, yes, that would be my Michaela. Her childhood was rough you see." He turns to Sloan, instinctively knowing where he stands, beside my right shoulder and next to Doran who is back to holding the glass containing the weird substance. "She could have turned out either way."

Understanding dawns on me in that moment. After Finn's arrest, Michaela pursued justice, but Sloan pursued the truth. All this time I thought it was Michaela's lack of some gift or talent like Bina, Sloan, and apparently Finn all have. But it's something much simpler than that. Single-minded dedication. Justice at any and all cost, even at the expense of the truth. I feel bad for her then, but only a little bit. She's still a total psycho.

"Now, my assistant will hand me the glass containing the memory mixture." Doran rolls his eyes, but hands the glass to Finn.

I feel excited. As if I really am about to witness a bit of magic. And not my mom's immortal-goddess-of-the-Universe-magic, but real mind-bending magic. He unties the leather cord, and slips the bullet off with deft fingers. He then lets the bullet fall into the glass where it immediately sinks into the strange substance. Finn moves the glass around, completely submerging the bullet in the silver goo.

"What is that stuff?" I ask.

But Finn only smiles. "A magician never reveals his secrets, my dear." Then a strange thing begins to happen. I can now see the bottom of the glass. The amount of the substance is decreasing right before our eyes.

"How is that..." Sloan says, eyes growing wide in wonder. I can only imagine what it was like having parents like Bina and Finn growing up.

"The bullet is absorbing the metallurgy. This is the memory stuff. It's actually more than just a metal, it has some living components. That's why we call it a living memory when it's infused with an object."

"Do I want to know what the living components are?" I ask.

But Doran vehemently shakes his head. "Trust me."

The small bullet absorbs the last of the strange substance. Using his fingers, Finn takes the bullet back out of the glass. It's not wet or anything. Nothing is strange or different about it. In fact it looks remarkably the same as before. Finn rethreads the leather cord through the bullet and hands it back to me. I lift my hair so that Sloan can retie the knot at the nape of my neck. His fingers brush against my Elemental Star tattoo and send a pleasant shiver through me.

"So how will it work?" I ask, although I think I may already know. But this is different. My mother's magic and Finn's are two very different kinds.

Finn waves a dismissive hand. "As you'd expect it to. The bullet is now infused with the memory of this place. You think it and if your thoughts are in alignment with what the bullet remembers it will bring you here. It's really rather simple. Law of attraction and all that."

"Right. Simple." I agree, but not agreeing at all really. Science was my worst subject. Well, actually, they were all my worst subject. I never was a very good student. You could even ask Sloan, since he was my Universal History teacher. I'm sure he'd agree. Ahna was always the good student. Li and I not so much.

"Finn?" I don't want to ask this question. It's something I'd rather not think about, but my mother had told me before that Finn was an invaluable source when it came to knowledge about the Imminent Darkness. "Li's sister, Ahna. Before I turned myself in, she died. She'd gotten infected with something. Something from the Imminent Darkness. An insect of some kind that got into her body and turned into her an incubator or something. It literally killed her from the inside out. After the swarm was harvested, it flew away toward the colony, as if it was programmed to do exactly that." My voice catches and Sloan puts a reassuring hand on my shoulder. Ahna was his friend too. "How?"

Finn closes his eyes and the impish smile that graced his face as he gave the bullet a living memory has been replaced with something more solemn.

"The Imminent Darkness is ancient, as I'm sure you know, Ka. It is as old as the Universe itself. And that's a very long time to exist. The amount of time provides many opportunities to travel to different galaxies and to different planets. The Imminent Darkness may only be energy—as all things that exist are—but it has had the millennia to learn many things. It has had many years to learn destruction. And to learn death."

Doran grows very still, now standing to Finn's left and holding the empty glass. I've never met Doran's dad. I know he was an Unbalanced Water. I know there was a lot of rage. I've seen it. In his memories. But I don't know what became of him. Just that he's no longer around. Doran seems to stiffen at the mention of death. But just as quickly as I noticed, he's seemed to revert back to a more relaxed posture. No one else seems to have noticed.

Finn continues. "I'd heard about the swarm. The guards in the prison…they talk too much. More than they should. After so long you learn how to listen not only to what they're saying, but to what they're leaving out. How long did it take your friend Ahna to become sick?"

"I've no idea really. It's hard to tell when exactly she became infected. Days or weeks?" I look at Sloan and he nods in agreement. I don't mention that it's also a bit difficult to have a sense of time when the time we have here on Xon 9 is not the same as the Elemental Abyss or The Lands. In the various lands, days could pass and we'd return home to find out we'd only been gone half a day.

"Perhaps, since your friend's infection was the original, the subsequent ones aren't quite as strong. Diseases can mutate with each generation."

"Mom said there's been signs. People who come from above more recently than us, said the hospital is full to capacity. They're complaining of fatigue and weakness, sallow complexions, can't keep any food down. One guy said he heard some patients were becoming so agitated and aggressive that they had to be locked down…"

Doran's voice trails off and I exchange a glance with Sloan.

Ahna was exactly the same way. She had become increasingly angry with me. I had thought, at the time, that she'd had every right. Who could blame her if she hated me after I am the one primarily responsible for draining her twin brother of his Fire and nearly killing him not once but twice? If it weren't for my mother and her quick thinking, Li surely would have died the second time. But instead of Li being angry, it had been her. Eventually, her anger subsided and she confessed to me that she didn't think I could win. That I wasn't enough to defeat the Imminent Darkness. I know now it's because she knew what it had in store, knew of the death and destruction that would slowly build around me until it reaches a crescendo of unprecedented proportions. Little does the ID know just what affect seeing my best friend die in front of my eyes would have on me.

"It still can take longer. Maybe something about your friend's physiology…" And then it's like watching a lightbulb go off over Finn's head. "That's it exactly! When did you begin the Transitional Phase?"

Doran shrugs. "Dunno. A few months ago?"

"That's why! Most likely, the majority of people who are being infected are full-blown Elemental, so it's taking longer for the disease to sicken them and to spread. Your friend still was only a Changeling, more human than Elemental. Therefore, it took significantly less time to have an effect on her."

"Has your mom heard word of any deaths from it yet?" Sloan asks. I can see the wheels turning in his head, he's begun to pace back and forth. Bina is still above ground.

Doran shakes his head. "No. Not yet. Just the usual. People getting sicker. The so-called Civil Law Enforcement creating mayhem."

"We need to find out," Finn says. "I need to know as much as possible. Has anyone come down recently who worked in the hospital? If so, we will need to quarantine them. But it will also give me a chance to collaborate on an antidote with some of the physicians and scientists down here."

"Roger that. I'll go find Mom and have her look over the recent in-takes forms. If anyone worked in the hospital then she would know." Doran sets down the empty glass and salutes Finn—even though he can't see it—before wandering back out of the small cavern and toward the rest of the tent city in search of Mrs. Chatfield.

My mind is reeling. I turn to Finn, suspicious. "I thought you just did research."

"Oh, my dear. I did do research. But I researched everything. Part of Universal Intelligence is knowing all of the ways that an attack could happen, either from the outside or the inside. That included researching nuclear, psychological and bio-warfare." For a moment Finn looks proud of the work that he's done, his chin is held high and there's the smallest of smiles on his lips. Except that same research—the same research that may save us all—is the same that got him locked up and tortured. Sometimes the Universe just seems so cruel. The small smile vanishes. "Let's hope that the rest of the colony can be spared the death that took your friend."

...

That evening, after a simple meal of soup and bread—much better than the rock-hard bread I'd been eating for the last month—I begin packing my bag for my final trip to the last of the Elemental lands. Since I willingly turned myself in, Sloan had kept my things.

Now, I sit on my cot in the glow of a small lantern, and sift through the contents of my messenger bag. It has two fang-holes from when the Imminent Darkness took the form of a wolf and attacked me. And it has a hole that was burned through by the Fire stone when it glowed white hot and I almost lost it. I toss a couple of empty water bottles aside and fish out the small mason jars that roll around inside. I hold one of the jars up to the light. It is filled with disgusting green gloop that makes me want to gag and throw up my dinner. Medeis Seaweed.

"What the heck is that?" Cerise asks making a face as she plops down on the end of the cot. Her red hair is braided across her forehead, then tumbling in waves to her shoulders. Her lips are pink, pouty and perfect and her skin is pearlescent and pale as porcelain. If she wasn't so damn fierce, her beauty alone would make me hate her. But I don't. Because let's be honest, any girl that will stab herself in the hip with a dagger in order to save someone she doesn't even know, is pretty badass in my book. And she knows how to shoot a bow and arrow. Oh, and she used to be a mermaid. On second thought, maybe I should be more jealous.

I look up. "Medeis Seaweed. You stuff it in your ears and it drowns out the death song of the Elemental Abyss. I noticed you're getting around fine on those human legs now." I set the jar down on a small table.

She leans back and kicks her long legs into the air, admiring them. "You know they really do grow on you after a time." She giggles, then sits upright. "What are those?"

I shake the second jar. Its bottom is full of tiny seeds. "Zephyrus Seeds to summon the wind." I set the jar next to the seaweed and take out the third jar. It has two brilliantly red blooms inside it. "And Ignis Flos. Fire Flower."

"And you need those things because..."

"The Elemental Abyss is not an easy trip. These are just some things that I've found that come in handy. Actually, my mom's the one who discovered they come in handy."

We're silent for a minute as I continue to rummage through my bag. I pull out a leather book with gold lettering: *The Five Goddesses*. The book in my dreams may be the story of my life, but this is the story of my mother's. Something that was mistaken for a fairy tale and passed on as legend, but is as every bit as truthful as a researched biographical history. Stuck inside it like a bookmark is the familiar ragged edges of my mom's hand-drawn map with her personal notes written in her sloppy, familiar scrawl. A lump forms in my throat. Things can never—will never—be the same again.

"Do you miss her?" Cerise asks. My cheeks redden from shame. Never once did I ask Cerise about her family or her parents. She wanted so badly to come home with us that she was willing to risk possible death, just to escape the Land of Water. I'd assumed it was because of my Aunt Tulia and what she'd done to Cerise's lover. But maybe that's not all Cerise was trying to escape.

I nod. "It's dumb though. It's not like she's…dead or anything. She's still alive. Just not here."

Cerise scoots closer to me and puts an arm around my sagging shoulders. She smells like warm, fresh-baked bread with a hint of sea breeze—the lingering effects of her previous life.

"I know exactly what you mean," she says softly. "When the Water Queen cursed Ridge, he was still there. Every day he was there and I was thankful he was alive, but for how much he was present for the Queen was how much he was absent to me. He was alive, just not here." Her fingers softly graze the space beneath her jacket that cover her heart.

"And now, you'll never see him." Somehow I know it's the most wrong of wrong things to say. And yet, I can't keep the words from tumbling from my lips.

"It's okay," Cerise says and I hear the same lump in her throat that threatens to boil over in mine. "Because I'd rather not. I'd rather remember him the way he was. The way he was before he was cursed. That Ridge—*my* Ridge—he is dead to me. That time in my life is dead to me now too." A single, perfect tear rolls down her cheek. "But just because part of us has died, doesn't mean that something new cannot—will not—grow in its place. We just have to let it bloom."

CHAPTER 9

My sleep was restless and dreamless. Sloan is shaking me awake and I assume it's morning, but when you're underground there's no real sense of time. Just the fabricated construct of keeping time.

I'm already dressed in jeans and a long-sleeved t-shirt. I shove my feet into some boots and run a brush through my hair, which has now grown almost to my collarbone, its edges jagged where Sloan cut them not so long ago. I snap a hair tie around my wrist and shove a sweater into my messenger bag. You never know what kind of weather you'll encounter in the various lands. Something gives me the impression that the Land of Metal might be a bit chilly.

The tent is now empty so I trudge to the meal area. Each morning a group of Earths—the most nurturing of the Elementals— bake fresh muffins, make porridge, and pour hot coffee. Everyone is already surrounding a small table: Sloan, Doran, Li, Cerise, Finn, and Bax. I never was much of a morning person. And I don't like not seeing the rise and set of the twin moons. In some ways I feel like I traded one prison for another. Don't get me wrong. I know that I'm free here and that I have my friends now. But until I can return to my true home, I can't help but feel a little bit trapped. So, despite the unknown, I'm thankful for my final trip to the Land of Metal.

"It's about time you joined us," Li says pushing a bran muffin and a cup of coffee in my direction.

"You know how I feel about mornings. It is morning, right?" I ask sitting down and picking a piece off the top of the muffin to shove into my mouth.

"No worries, my little firecracker. You'll be out into the world soon enough risking life and limb to save the world," Sloan assures me.

I grin. "I wouldn't want it any other way."

I know that sometimes my brazenness frightens Sloan. Not because it makes it harder for him to fulfill his Everlasting Vow, but because I know that one of his greatest fears is to lose me. He once told me it wasn't the immortal part of me he was worried about, but the mortal part. However, he seems to forget that despite any gifts and talents, he is one-hundred-percent mortal and therefore one-hundred-percent capable of death. And if I didn't take brazen risks there's a good chance that he'd end up one-hundred-percent dead.

"So, just to recap one more time…?" Doran raises an eyebrow at Finn even though he can't see it. But he seems to sense that the question is aimed at him. An empty bowl of porridge sits in front of him and he's holding a cup of coffee with both hands.

"Indeed. You five will have to join hands in order for the memory object to transport all of you at once. Now, don't forget that you may see one another's memories as you travel through the space-time continuum. That's completely normal."

And don't I know it. I've seen Doran's memories, and Sloan's, even my mother's. I've never shared what I've seen, but I can only imagine what they've seen of my own.

Finn continues. "Now, this memory object is unique. It's absorbed the memory of Metal on an energetic level. Once you're in the periphery, the necklace should latch onto the unique energetic frequency of the Metal and transport you to the place with the highest probable matching frequency."

"I hate to be the downer of the party, but what if it doesn't take us to where we want to go?" asks Li.

Finn looks thoughtful. "Well, that's definitely a possibility, but given that the Land of Metal is an entire world—assumedly within our Universe, then it should have the highest vibrational match. That is the object's last memory. But once you leave here and reach the Land of Metal, this place will be its last living memory. It always takes on the memory of the last place it was, then it matches the frequency and transports you accordingly. In theory, this should allow you to completely bypass the Elemental Abyss."

"In theory?" I ask. I know Finn did his best and that his talent in these matters far surpasses anyone else's maybe besides my mother, and I'm no scientist, but theory does not imply guarantee.

Finn shifts uncomfortably in his seat and his unseeing eyes find me and rest on my face. And even though it's impossible and he is blind now, I feel like he can actually *see* me. That he can see the worry etched across my brow and the sadness reflected in my eyes. Somehow he knows my unspoken concerns: that it won't be enough, that too many things can go wrong, that the cost of life is too high for only a theory.

"Ka. I've done the best that I can. Within all reason, it should work perfectly. But, as with all things, there are risks. I do not want to lead you into something—excuse the pun—blindly." Finn's voice is calm and reassuring. He reaches across Sloan and puts a warm hand over mine. "Make no mistake. I, more than most, know what this mission means to you, to us, to the entire colony. I would not take a foolish risk on something of such great significance."

I nod, then remembering just how willing he was in the past to take risks, say, "I know. I'm sorry for questioning you, Finn."

"No apologies. By all means you have every right to question me. If anyone has the most at stake here, it is you."

I nod again and the conversation continues, but I find myself no longer listening. The voices around me become nothing but a background buzz in my head. I've felt angered, and emboldened, and even frightened, but this is a different feeling that sits heavily with me, like a lead weight in the pit of my stomach. I want to succeed, but no one's ever gotten something just for the wanting. If I don't succeed, not only is my entire colony in jeopardy, but we are the only ones to inhabit this small planet. And on a grander scale, as if that wasn't nauseating enough, the Imminent Darkness has infiltrated the various lands, and it has roamed the Universe in its quest for so-called balance. A balance that was tipped, and threw the whole Universe out of whack simply because I was born. If I don't succeed, what happens to the rest of the Universe? What will happen to my mother and her sisters? To all the people and creatures I've met in my travels to the other lands? Nahele, Qildor, and Hennie. Ridge. Nightfall. Will they all just cease to exist because I failed?

The muffin rolls in my stomach and I suddenly feel like I'm going to be sick. I rise quickly from the table and dash behind the stacked stone ovens, back where no one can see me. It's quiet and the buzzing inside my head begins to subside. I press my forehead to the cool rock of the cavern wall and take deep, slow breaths. In and out. In and out.

One step at a time, Kata. One damn step at a time. It's all I have right now, and it will have to do. The nauseous feeling begins to subside, but I don't think I'll be eating any more bran muffins any time soon.

I hear footsteps behind me and I automatically assume that it's Sloan. "I'm fine," I say, eyes still closed, forehead still pressed against the smooth coolness.

"You said it not me."

Li. He comes over and stands beside me, leaning his back against the wall face, so that he's looking in the opposite direction at the ovens. Truth be told, Li isn't necessarily my first choice of comfort. And I'm admittedly a bit surprised it isn't Sloan standing here instead.

As if reading my mind, Li explains. "You need tough love right now, Kata. Not *frou-frou* love."

I cringe and look at him sideways. "We are not *frou-frou*."

"Ooooh, Water Man, I love yooooou so much." He makes his voice all high-pitched in a horribly inauthentic impression of me. Despite myself, I laugh because it's so horrible.

"See told you. Tough love."

I scowl. "I've had tougher."

He nods conceding. "Okay. Well, you've forced my hand. I was trying to play nice. I know what you're thinking and I want you to know that you're wrong. I know you didn't ask for this—and neither did I and sure as heck, neither did Ahna—but it's the reality of the situation. And yes, you are one girl and the Imminent Darkness is vast and terrifying—damn, terrifying and I like to think after all that's happened to me I know that just as well as you do. But you know what? You're not in this alone, Kata. And that's what will make all the difference in the world. People believe in you. Sloan and the others believe in you. *I* believe in you and Ahna did too."

This is by far one of the longest speeches I've probably ever heard pour from Li's mouth. Especially one that didn't involve any provocation from the Black Bazaar.

"Ahna didn't think I could do it." Is the dumb thing that I say in response. "She told me so."

"You know as well as I do, that it wasn't her talking at the end. It was him—or it or whatever *it* is—that wanted you to think that. Not Ahna." He looks down at his boots. "We all make mistakes, Kata.

But it's learning from them that marks the difference between success and failure."

I nod because he's right of course. And even though he's the last person I would expect such wisdom from, a lot has happened to Liwald Sollomon in the last few months. Most of it unpleasant, but I can't say that he hasn't become a better person despite it.

"Thanks." I push myself off the wall and turn so that I'm facing him. I want to hug him, but it seems strange now, what with me and Sloan and him and Cerise, so I settle for shoving him in the shoulder instead. "I needed that."

"I know you did. I could see it on your face. But really, I did it because about-to-spew-bran-muffins-all-over-the-breakfast-table-puke-face is not a good look on you."

This time I shove him harder, but I'm still smiling.

. . .

The forest is dark and dense. The smell of soil and rot fills my nostrils. The five of us are alone, outside the hidden entrance to the tent city that is some number of meters below our feet. The red sun of Xon 9 is blazing bright and the constant breeze rustles the silvery leaves of the trees. Their bark is thick and dark. It's so early that the twin moons are low in the sky as they appear to set.

If we were within the colony and not out here near the periphery, everything would have a reddish-tint to it. At night, it becomes pinker as the sky darkens and the white of the twin moons casts their glow. But in the forest everything is cast in shadows from the trees that tower above us, forming a canopy over our heads.

"Are we ready?" I ask.

Doran nods and takes my hand. I can't help but feel as though we've come full circle. He unexpectedly started this journey with me and now we're going to finish it. Together. I hope.

Sloan comes over and takes my free hand, then Cerise takes his, and finally Li stands between Cerise and Doran. I look at their faces. Sloan's expression is one of silent determination. Cerise looks like she's about ready for the ride of her life, and I suppose she is having spent the last seventeen years in a land made of water. As I turn to Li, I realize with a jolt I no longer feel the knot in my stomach at the black, tribal-like tattoo that marks his face. The result of his Fire being drained from him. He once accused me of looking at him like he was broken, but now, despite everything that's happened, all I see in him is strength. Lastly, I glance at Doran whose face is expressionless more or less, but whose dark brown eyes are dancing with excitement. I could not ask for better companions on this journey.

"You may feel disoriented and get flashes of memories from one another," I remind everyone. At various points each has traveled with me, but the feeling of violating the time space continuum is like no other I've ever experienced. "Okay, then. Here we go."

I close my eyes and imagine a cold, metallic place. The bullet necklace around my neck seems to pulsate as I try to envision the last stone, a stone made of hematite. And as soon as I think it, I feel myself being pulled up and out. The forest around me quickly fades and everything goes black.

I see nothing and I hear nothing. It's like traveling in a vacuum. There is nothingness all around me. It is both terrifying and wonderful. I feel as though I'm being thrown forward into a deep lake and there's no bottom in sight.

Memories begin to flash through my mind. This is always the part I hate the most. I see myself, but through Sloan's eyes. Only everything appears fuzzy. I can feel the weight of a body beneath me and when I look down I see Tullia's face, her long blonde hair spread out and around her head in a halo, lavender eyes hungry. Her ruby lips are curled into a devious smile as she strokes the side of my face and murmurs something to me. My stomach coils at the memory, recognizing it as when I found Sloan under Tullia's spell. And then the image disappears and is replaced with something new. I'm staring down at myself lying on the cot in the tent city. My face is drawn, pale, and cheeks sunken in. My eyelids flutter rapidly and my forehead is dewy with sweat. I see Sloan's fingers—my fingers—press a cold towel to my forehead. I can feel the worry and confusion coalescing inside him. The rage at his sister.

The image slips away and is replaced with a different one. I feel the familiarity of Sloan fade away, replaced with something more volatile. Quick to anger, but also quick to help. I feel a soft, squishiness and look down at my hands. I'm kneading dough to make bread. A woman beside me knicks my chin with her knuckles and says something while smiling. Then the image is replaced with another of me being knocked down over and over. I look up and see Bax towering over me. His expression isn't one of malice, but I can feel the dislike brewing inside me. My lip is bleeding and my muscles all ache as if they're on fire. But Bax barks something at me and I'm automatically pushing myself up ready for another round.

After the last image of Doran training with Bax, they begin to come faster and faster until they're so rapid, they're nothing but a blur and I can't make heads or tails out of anything. We fly through the nothingness until I see a single, bright pinprick of light as if at the end of a long tunnel. The light grows brighter and larger until we are hurled through it in a moment of blinding brightness.

We have arrived.

CHAPTER 10

As we tumble through the portal I lose my grip on Doran's hand and land on something hard like stone. I struggle to catch my breath, pulling sensation back to me. I can still feel Sloan's hand in mine. I slowly sit up. All the blood seems to rush to my head and I feel slightly dizzy for a minute. My brain cloudy with the stream of memories.

"Ugh. You could have warned us again about the landing," Li groans rolling onto his side. And that's when I realize why the landing was even more painful than usual. We've landed on a cliff edge of solid rock. I'm surprised nobody seems to have broken anything.

Sloan pushes himself to a seated position beside me. I tentatively stand up to take in our new surroundings. I never know where exactly the Elemental stones will be located. Sometimes I feel drawn in a particular direction—like a lost part of me calling me back home—and other times I meet nice people, and I use the term people loosely, who are willing to help me on my journey. But it doesn't seem like there's a lot of people around here.

Above me the sky is charcoal gray with thick black clouds. In the sky hangs a peculiar, crescent-shaped purple moon. So deep in color it would appear almost indigo. Strange silver lights are sprinkled throughout the sky and my first instinct is to call them stars, and yet they seem to dance across the sky more than they seem to glow. Past the cliff edge, is a tumultuous looking gray sea, with huge, crashing waves. There's no beach of pink sand like in the Land of Earth, and the waves violently throw themselves against the cliff face.

I turn in a slow semi-circle. Behind where we landed is a jagged mountain. A narrow path winds up it and leads through a range of ominous looking peaks. In the distance I can see a building, tall and metallic, shining silver in the light of the strange silver stars. I see three towers, each rounded at the top. The gray sky is reflected in its metallic sides.

I point. "I think we should start there."

Sloan is standing now and he follows my finger to the distant building. "Looks like a castle or fortress of some type."

"Probably Aunt Isa's house," I shrug.

Li is wrapping a linen bandage around one of Cerise's hands. Apparently, she cut her palms on the rough rock when we landed. But otherwise, everyone appears more or less in one piece. I start toward the narrow path, which forces us to walk single file as the jagged cliff face pushes against us on one side and the violent waves crash far below us on the other.

We don't go but a few yards when there's a sudden, deafening crash and the entire charcoal sky lights up in a menacing white light. It's quickly followed by a boom so loud that it shakes the mountainside to our left. Even after it's over I can still feel the buzz in my ears.

"What the heck was that?" Cerise's scared voice rises over the buzz.

"Lightning," I explain.

"And thunder," Sloan adds.

"Is a storm coming?" Doran asks.

We don't have surface precipitation on Xon 9. But in this land, there is a sea and the sky has a bruised appearance about it. Rain would not make the journey to the towers any more easy, that's for sure.

Sloan closes his eyes and inhales the saltiness of the air. It's windy up this high, and his shaggy brown hair whips around his face. He shakes his head and opens his eyes, which are blazing a brilliant emerald green.

"No. No storms are coming. I think...I think it's just part of this land. It feels different. Don't you feel it too?" At first I figure he's just talking his wonky talk, you know dream-walking and mind-reading. But then I realize that he's right.

The buzzing in my ears hasn't stopped. After the thunder faded away, a high-pitched buzz still remains.

"Different how?" Li asks. "Like, *oh you got new glasses, that's different.* Or like, *oh the entire place has been taken over by the Imminent Darkness, that's different.* Those are two very different differents."

Sloan grins. "The former, I think. It feels...like energy. But not negative energy like the Imminent Darkness."

"The ID feeds off energy. If this place is full of energy, I'm surprised it hasn't come here yet. It would be like a smorgasbord," I say.

"You and your fancy words," Li chastises. As if in response, another jagged scar of lightning clashes against the charcoal sky. It's followed by a low rumble.

"Let's keep going," Doran encourages from behind me, nudging me forward with his shoulder. "If this energy ends up being some bad juju, I don't want to stick around to find out."

...

It seems like we walk for hours down the winding path. The wind whips my hair and burns my cheeks. Long ago, I put on the sweater that I'd brought with me. Lightning continues to crash all around us and my ears buzz with the energy that is this land. It's unlike anything I've ever experienced. Sure, each land had its own uniqueness. Fire was all brimstone, Earth was natural and beautiful, Wood was mysterious and full of magical beings, and Water was full of more magical creatures, but of the darker variety. This is different.

It feels dark with a side of foreboding, almost like I can feel something being stirred up. Only I can't tell if it's an actual feeling, or just the effect of all the energy crashing around me. My feet are aching inside my boots and the calf muscle of my right leg cramped up after only about an hour of walking, my muscles still unused to the exertion despite the last couple days of training. Several times I've stumbled only for Doran to catch me from behind.

Finally, after what seems like forever, the path seems to widen. The path winds down into a valley of jagged rocks. We're standing on a small crest somewhat even with the top of the towers and below in a small valley is the sprawling building. The entire building is made of steel and glass and it sparkles in the starlight and glows silver-gold in the flash of the lightning. The building consists of the three towers, all of varying heights. Now that we're closer I can see better that they're rounded at the top and seem to spiral into the air. No light emits from the building's inside, and if not for the strangeness of this place, under other circumstances I would have thought that it was abandoned.

"Do you think we go there?" asks Cerise nodding her chin toward the towers. I nod. "Do you think the stone is there?"

"No. But I think Isa is. And I think Isa can tell us where to find the Metal stone." Lightning blazes and thunder booms, cutting off the word *stone*.

Doran comes up beside me. "I know I grew up Metal and all, but I'm not sure I like this place. Something feels weird about it."

No one says anything, all in agreement by our silence. I edge my way onto the path leading down into the valley and the others follow. I am not brave. Nor am I a risk-taker. Before this whole ordeal even started, I was almost painfully ordinary. I stuck to the shadows and I blended in. I wasn't exceptionally good at anything in particular, just okay at a lot of things. And if you told me I was some girl from a passed down legend, chances are I would have laughed in your face. I didn't ask for any of this. But it's the card I've been dealt, and I've learned to pretend that I'm a lot of things that I'm not.

Like pretending I wasn't lonely or pretending that I'm no longer afraid. Or pretending that I'm not going to somehow royally screw up this whole ordeal. But the funny thing about pretending, is the more that you do it the more convincing you become. Even to yourself.

That's why now I boldly head down the rocky path, my boots slipping and sliding on the loose rocks. I occasionally grab a jutting boulder to slow down my descent. The location of the towers is peculiar. Surrounded by a sea and a range of perilous mountains, set deep in a valley, seemingly isolated.

As we get closer to the towers it somehow seems to grow darker. My eyes adjust quickly, but I can feel something moving around us. I pause and listen, but only silence greets me. Still, I can't shake the feeling that there's something moving in the shadows. There's another flash of lightning, but in the valley its brilliant light doesn't reach all the crevices and we're still cast in shadow while the sky is momentarily lit up like a torch. In the valley the wind has gone still and there's an eeriness surrounding the towers.

I stop when I reach the jagged rocks at the bottom of the valley. I lean over and gently press my finger tip to one of them and a drop of blood instantly forms on my finger tip. They're much too sharp to simply climb across. I can't foresee a way around them and they'd be much too dangerous to climb them. It's like some kind of rock dagger moat.

"What now, Princess?" Li asks, taking in the acres of jagged rock that block our path to the base of the towers.

I shrug. "I was hoping you'd have an idea or two. Or five."

"Well, I…" But his reply is drowned out by a loud humming coming from the direction of the towers.

Seemingly out of nowhere, a black disc comes floating across the gray sky, but as it gets closer, I can see that it's really a small ship of some kind. It moves quickly and easily, staying low as it seems to glide above the jagged rocks.

Sloan shoots me a worried glance and again I shrug. I've never quite seen anything like it. Our technology at home…in eight-hundred years we've progressed so little. Some technology has far surpassed others, but some things have stayed painfully unremarkable thanks to the Imminent Darkness. No one likes being oppressed without even knowing. Actually, I think that may be the worst kind.

We stand there in a kind of awe, as the ship glides toward us then seems to stop, hovering in space only a few yards away, before it lowers itself onto a space of flat rock. There's a *whoosh* as the ship seems to power down and then a *hiss* as a door opens and a man—no, a creature—steps out of the door.

The creature-man is tall, so tall that I have to crane my head back just to take all of him in. He walks toward us, but his feet make no sound. He is thin with gangly arms and legs, and appears to be naked. I immediately think of rudimentary images of aliens from Old Earth thousands of years ago. His skin is dark—almost charcoal like the sky—and his head is round and bald. His eyes are oval-shaped, but completely black with no color. His face has no noticeable nose or mouth and the effect is disconcerting at best. White, metallic lines zigzag across his skin, but as I stare in wonder the lines suddenly shift and change, resembling the jagged lines of lightning across the sky. They remind me of the metallic threads that web across the Metal Elementals' faces.

"Greetings, I am Oosa." The creature says, only he has no mouth. So I'm not exactly sure how he said it. I glance at Sloan whose eyes have grown wide.

"Telepathy," he whispers. "He's communicating directly into our minds. Manipulating our brain waves to a different energetic frequency."

"Very good, Human Boy." The voice sounds slightly robotic, but there's a hint of approval. He turns, black eyes focused on me. "You and your companions will come with me. Queen Isa has been waiting for your arrival."

I narrow my eyes. "How do I know that I can trust you?" I ask.

If it's one thing that I've learned from these trips, it is trust no one until they can prove themselves trustworthy. Or until they save your life. Whichever happens to come first.

"Silly girl. You do not trust the Queen's most highly-ranked of advisors?" The white lines on his skin coalesce and shift. There's a burst of lightning and a cluster of lines on the right side of his chest glow brilliantly white before fading away. This creature—Oosa—somehow is connected to the energy of this land. "Everything is energy, niece-of-my-queen."

"Hey!" I frown. "I didn't give you permission to do that."

He bows his head slightly. "My apologies. It's a fortunate side-effect of matching frequencies."

Frequencies. Finn had talked about energetic frequencies when he inserted the memory into the bullet of my necklace. My hair stands on end with the realization that Finn Braden may know much more than I ever thought he did. Now, I know why the Leadership Council feared him so.

"Come, Queen Isa does not like to be kept waiting." Oosa turns his back and heads toward the ship, fully expecting us to follow him.

"Yeah, and neither do Water Queens or Fairy Kings. In fact, you whole lot are an impatient bunch." I grumble, but I step forward to follow Oosa.

Doran grabs my elbow. "Are you sure, Ka?" His brow is furrowed and his eyes are worried.

"Of course not," I reply honestly. I glance back at the jagged rocks and the looming towers so close, yet so far away. "But what choice do we have?"

Doran stares at me a moment, as if searching my face for something, then deciding that he finds it he releases my elbow, and with his head down follows after Oosa. I scurry after them, careful not to slip on the rocks. Cerise, Li, and Sloan bring up the rear, hurrying across the loose rocks toward the ship. I wonder how we're all going to fit in a ship that seems so small. Then I wonder how Oosa himself, towering over us, fit into a ship that small. *At least it's a quick trip*, I think.

. . .

Inside, the ship is aglow in a soft purple light coming from various control panels and instruments. The ship is bigger than it looks due to a deep area in its center that's sunken in and has plush, purple benches curved around it.

"Make yourself comfortable," Oosa says. The others sit tentatively on the benches, staring around in awe at the sleek interior of the ship. And I know what they're thinking because I'm thinking the exact same thing. This should be us. After 800 plus years, we should be flying around Xon 9 in ships just like this one. Only we're not.

I ignore Oosa's command to make myself comfortable and instead follow him to the front of the ship where there are a bunch of important looking knobs and levers. Somehow, it gives me the urge to touch every single one, but I don't. Beyond the steering instruments is a narrow slit of a window and outside of it I can see where we were just standing. The mountain peaks climb into the charcoal sky and the strange silver stars and purple moon hanging above. Lightning flashes, but inside the ship I hear no sound. I watch as the land is momentarily lit up in white. I give a little gasp. It's both peculiar and magnificent. The lightning reflects off the gray clouds and reverberates through the sky in fractured snippets.

116

I feel myself thrown off balance as the ship lifts off from the ground. Oosa moves his long, slender fingers along the controls swiftly as if he's done it a million times before. For all I know he has. We're soon gliding over the sharp rocks that surround the towers, easing into an ascent. We fly low around the towers, then almost as soon as we started, we begin an abrupt drop into what would appear to be a bit of smooth rock at the base of the largest tower. I grip the dashboard beneath the window, confused as to why we aren't just making a gentle landing as Oosa had before, when suddenly the ground opens like a pair of gaping jaws and swallows us whole.

We glide through the darkness, until the ship levels out. We're greeted by bright silver lights that reveal we're in a tunnel. The ship sails slowly forward and the tunnel opens onto a cavernous room. There are several black ships like the one we currently occupy, lined up around the large space. Oosa glides us into an open space between two identical ships. Then presses a lever. The ship momentarily hovers before carefully lowering itself to the ground.

"That was interesting," I say still gripping the dashboard, my knuckles white.

"Most people enjoy that the first time." Oosa's voice sounds as if it is smiling. "Come, Queen Isa doesn't like to be kept waiting." He repeats his words from earlier.

He stalks away, black body crackling with white lightning, and we follow him back out of the ship door.

The space is obviously some kind of hangar. There's at least ten ships and I wonder why Isa would need them. Does she fly out past her land? Or is her land so vast that there are other communities that she must travel to?

"Both." Oosa answers reading my mind. I don't hide my dislike for him doing so. "Our ships can fly out into the Universe, but also the Land of Metal is a vast one with tumultuous terrain. It is easiest to fly in the safety of our ships then to traverse across the mountains and the sea."

"Well, you can't argue with that logic," Doran says, running a finger along the gray stone wall of the cavern. When he pulls his finger away there's a filmy smudge of gray. He shrugs and wipes his finger off on his cargo pants.

Oosa leads us through a sliding metal door. It doesn't have a keypad and I'm not sure if he used telepathy to open it or if it just opened because there is a sensor in the floor. We continue down another hallway which dead ends into a glass elevator. Again, the door slides open and the six of us squeeze inside. It's not very large, especially with Oosa's massive form. But somehow we all fit, standing shoulder to shoulder and back to stomach. The door slides shut and my stomach gives a little jolt as we nimbly move upward.

The elevator carries us through some kind of tunnel system, so the view isn't much to look at it as we move up and down, and left to right. It's all just smooth, rounded out gray stone. My stomach rolls with each change in direction and I hear Sloan groan behind me as we start moving to the right and then abruptly head upwards. Good thing no one's ate in a while.

Finally, the elevator comes to a stop. Through the glass I can see a magnificent hallway. Its ceiling is arched and supported with steel beams that gleam in the dim light of wall sconces. The doors slide open and I follow Oosa onto a black marble floor with a plush silver runner down its length.

"Fancy," Li mumbles as he steps off the elevator.

The light inside the sconces seem to bounce and dance. Casting strange shadows across the walls that give the illusion that the walls are moving like living things.

"Starlight," Oosa explains with a wave of a midnight-colored hand. "Much more energy efficient."

We reach the end of the hallway and a large set of shiny, metal doors greet us at its end. A creature that looks exactly like Oosa stands sentry, hands resting at his side. His black eyes don't make any move to indicate he's noticed us. A length of awkward silence stretches between us, then the guard bows to Oosa and grabs the handle of the door on the right, pulling it open with what seems a great deal of effort. I realize as I follow Oosa through the doorway, that some sort of telepathic exchange must have taken place.

The room in which we enter is opulent. The silver runner continues down more shiny black marble. Metallic walls are adorned with swaths of black, silver, and purple fabric. Instead of sconces though, above us the ceiling is jet black and it twinkles like the sky outside with the bizarre silver stars. If I didn't know that we were indoors, I would think that we were outside looking up, only there's no moon in here. Occasionally, there's a streak of thin, white-silver light that creates a scar across the pristine black. The room would be dimly lit, if not for the billions of pinpricks of light floating above our heads.

This place is so very unlike my mother's castle in the Land of Earth which is all brilliant white stone and vibrant colored-stained glass. Behind the castle she has a gorgeous garden with every bloom imaginable, and a beautiful pagoda. It's a place of serenity. But this place feels alive, as if it is crackling with energy just waiting to be released. The buzzing in my ears has become steadier and higher-pitched.

At the end of the runner is a metal dais with an elaborately constructed metal chair upholstered in black velvet. The throne is flanked by two, tall silver sculptures in jagged, organic shapes. Behind the throne are also two more creatures, again identical in appearance to Oosa. Charcoal skin like the sky, long arms and legs, ridiculously tall, absent facial features save for fathomless black eyes.

But the most peculiar thing is who sits on the throne. A beautiful woman sits draped across it, her legs thrown over one arm. Her obsidian hair flows down past her waist and pools around the base of the chair. She's wearing black leather leggings with glittery, silver pumps whose heals could probably stab someone to death. Her skin is pale—so pale it almost appears translucent—and it seems to shimmer and glow in the same way as the strange stars. Her top is long-sleeved and made of the same black leather as her leggings. Around her neck is an angular silver choker, much like the sculptures that flank her throne.

Her face is angular as well, with high cheekbones and deep,

indigo-colored lips. She's holding a scepter in her hand, a black stick with a metallic sphere at the end. Her nails are filed to points and painted black. She looks bored. As we approach the metal dais, Oosa pauses and I hear him say, "Your Majesty, your guests have arrived." He bows slightly.

The queen languidly takes us in, and I can only assume that we—I—probably are not quite what she had expected. Her eyes settle on me and I startle when I notice that her eyes, like Oosa's and the others, are coal black. The difference being, in the queen's eyes I see little cracks and flashes of white, as if her eyes have lighting inside them. As a daughter of Raj and Katayun, the Metal Goddess is almost as old as the Universe itself. But even in all her eccentricity, she would not appear much older than I am.

She sits upright in the throne, kicking her legs around. Her long hair sways around her with the sudden motion. And in her hair I see strands of silver. Isa stands, her long body unfolding gracefully until she towers above us, and not just because she is standing on the dais. She is easily a full head taller than Oosa. She steps off the dais and approaches me, extending a pale hand and dragging a pointed, black fingernail gently down the side of my face. Her expression is curious, but her eyes are completely unreadable. She peers around me at Cerise, Doran, Li, and Sloan then her eyes settle back on me. Her indigo lips curl into a smile, revealing a row of perfect, white teeth.

"Welcome, my niece. I have been waiting for you."

CHAPTER 11

We follow Isa into something she calls a receiving room. The ceiling isn't as majestic in here—I guess the throne room is going for the wow factor. In here, it's just high, arched, and metal. It gleams as if someone gets up on a ladder daily and shines it until they see their reflection in it. Perhaps that's another of Oosa's jobs.

Instead of the sconces, a large chandelier hangs from the ceiling. Like the sculptures in the throne room, it's twisted and organic, round spheres of glass contain the silvery light. Beneath the chandelier there's a small, round, glass table with a large, metal bowl on top of it. Around the table are two small couches and two chairs upholstered in a soft purple color. The floor is black marble with a plush silver area rug beneath the table and chairs.

Isa's heels sink into the soft rug and she makes her way to one of the chairs. She gestures to the couches and the five of us sit down.

"You're dismissed, Oosa. Thank you for your service," she says. Her voice is gentle and feminine, contrasting with her over-the-top appearance.

"My Queen," Oosa replies and then bows before going back out the door and closing it behind him.

"Those Fulgurs are so formal," Isa says rolling her black eyes. "Sometimes they can be such a drag."

I raise an eyebrow and glance at Sloan, who's sitting beside me, his knee reassuringly pressed into mine. He gives a slight shrug.

"You don't like them?" I ask. "The Fulgurs?" The name sounds strange in my mouth. *Full-gurrs.*

She waves a pale hand dismissively. "They're great. Very loyal. Very smart. Not necessarily the bravest, but I have the Tonitrui for that."

"Tonitrui?" Li asks, emphasizing each of the words' parts. *Tahn-i-true-ee.*

Isa smiles again. "You'll meet them soon enough." She crosses her legs and clasps her hands beneath her pointy chin. Her scepter lays on the table in front of her. "It's just been so long since I had guests that were my age."

I bite my lip and try not to laugh. "I hate to break it to you, Aunt Isa, but you have at least thousands of years on us."

Isa's indigo lips form a pout. "Well, I don't *feel* thousands of years old. Everyone around here is just as old as I am. They can be so *dull.*"

"This place seems anything but dull," Sloan points out. And he's right. With its flashes of lightning, booming thunder, and strange purple moon, this land seems mysterious. And possibly dangerous.

"True. To an outsider. But, like you said, after thousands of years you discover all there is to discover. Besides, it was created for me, so there isn't anything here that isn't a reflection of myself in one way or another." Her eyes flash briefly and there's the distant boom of thunder.

"This place seems strange. Ever since we've arrived, my ears haven't stopped buzzing," I tell her.

She nods as if it's perfectly natural. "Your human ears aren't used to the energetic frequency of this land. The sea that takes up at least two-thirds of this planet is positively charged. The charcoal sky is negatively charged, the two meet and—" she claps her hands— "the result is a buzzing in your ears and a whole lot of lightning."

"What about Oosa—the Fulgurs?" Cerise asks. "They're whole body appears to be lightning."

"Same concept, smaller scale. Everything is energy. People, places, things. All of it. That saying opposites attract exists for a reason. Which leads me to why you're here." She points at me. "*You* are the opposite of the Imminent Darkness. All the negative things that it represents, are the opposite of the things that you represent— to me, my sisters, your own people—and that is why it is so attracted to you."

"Lucky me," I mumble.

"Yes, lucky you. Some girls have all the fun." I would think she was joking, but there's no humor to her voice at all.

"The problem is, that silly Anuja threw everything out of whack when she went and fell in love with your father. I am a bit of a sucker for a good romance story, but the Imminent Darkness isn't so much a fan. It feeds on chaos and destruction. On death. But you—when you were born—there was so much love. From your parents, from all of us—your mother's sisters, even Raj and Katayun. You were bestowed with many gifts. And the Imminent Darkness hated you for it. And yet, that same hate is what drew it to you, like a moth to a flame."

She stops talking to reach across the table. She pulls the large, metal bowl toward her. Now that I'm seated beside her, I can see that the bowl is full of a watery, silver liquid that swirls peacefully around of its own accord. It reminds me of the stuff Finn created for the living memory. Like molten metal.

"What's that?" Doran asks, eyeing the liquid suspiciously.

"It allows me to see."

"Are you blind?" Li asks, confused.

"Not see literally. To see…beyond." She frowns, obviously not liking having to explain herself.

She picks up her scepter and holds it over the bowl's contents. First, she moves it in a counterclockwise direction and the liquid immediately swirls in the same direction. After several passes, she pauses and begins to move the scepter in the opposite direction. All the while she stares intently at the liquid, her coal-colored eyes intense, the silver liquid reflecting like discs inside them.

We all grow quiet as we watch the strange ritual. Isa's lips move but no sound comes out. All I can hear is Sloan's even breath and the buzzing in my ears, until after several long minutes Isa seems to snap out of her trance and looks up from the bowl of liquid.

"I don't know the exact location of the stone, but I do know who can help you to find it. The Chief Tonitrui will be able to lead you to it. Tonitrui aren't always trustworthy, that's why I don't keep them as my advisors and servants. They stay in the land on the other side of the sea."

"Are they dangerous?" Sloan asks.

Isa shakes her head, a thin strand of silver parting from the many black ones. "Not particularly. Just deceptive. And they will expect something in return for helping you to find the stone. Be careful that they don't trick you into promising something dear to you. They have a cunning way with words."

"How will we get to this land on the other side of the sea?" Cerise asks.

"I will have Oosa prepare a ship for you. It's relatively easy to navigate. The stone will not be easy to find if the Tonitrui are involved," Isa frowns and swirls her scepter over the liquid again, the metal sphere nearly kissing its surface. But then she decides better of it, and shakes her head. "Not only are the Tonitrui cunning and deceptive, they're also our land's best warriors."

"Sounds like a plan for success," Li mumbles and Cerise elbows him in the ribs.

Isa's solemn expression slips away, suddenly replaced with something bright. "We shall have a party! Tonight, in celebration of your journey!" She claps her hands excitedly. "And then we shall have another party upon your safe return!" She lowers her voice conspiratorially. "That is, if you do return safely."

Her mood swings seem a bit unpredictable. First, I thought she was going to be cruel like Tullia. She sure looked the part, but then she turned all business to discuss our visit, only to turn around and giggle like a teenager at being able to throw not one, but two parties. Well, possibly two parties. But I try not to think about that part. I see now where the Metals back home may get their spontaneity and temperament.

"I'll have Oosa set to work immediately on preparing our best ship for you. I'll even have him preload the coordinates to take you to the Isle of Tonitrui. I don't know if they're expecting you, but perhaps I can send word to the Chief. Now, you five must go and rest. I have a party to plan and my guests of honor need to look their best. After all, if you don't it's a poor reflection on my hospitality and we can't have that." Isa babbles on and on. I think I started tuning out at the word party.

My colony—no, my entire planet—is in danger and here we are taking naps and getting ready for a party. I have to remind myself that it's irrelevant. That time here is different than the time back home. What could be three days here, could be only hours back home. One—or two—parties won't matter in the long run.

The door to the receiving room opens, and Oosa appears having been summoned silently.

"Oosa, be a dear and show my niece and her friends to their

chambers. They must rest because I decided that tonight we shall have a party that will send them on their journey in style. After you see them to their chambers, I'd like for you to prepare our best ship for their use. Plug in the coordinates for the Isle of Tonitrui. Be sure it's well-fueled and stocked with provisions for their journey." She flips her long black hair over a bony shoulder and turns toward me. "Now, go and rest, darling niece, because I have a party to plan!"

. . .

We exit out of another glass elevator onto an even higher floor than the one where the throne room was located. Oosa leads us down another opulent hallway, with metal walls and a metal ceiling. Sconces line the wall and the floor is still black marble. There are several metal doors along either wall—almost invisible except for their barely decipherable door frames and a small glowing button beside each one. Oosa pauses in front of a door to our right. He presses the glowing button and the metal door slides into the wall, revealing a spacious room with three beds covered in rich black fabrics. The foot of the beds form a circle in the center of the room and a chandelier similar to the one in the receiving room hangs from the ceiling above them.

Oosa bows slightly. "For the gentlemen."

The guys exchange a look, bid us good-bye, and disappear into the cavernous room. The door sliding closed behind them. Cerise and I follow Oosa past a couple of more doors before he stops at another door on the right. Again, he presses the glowing button and the door slides open, disappearing into the metal wall.

"And for the ladies." He gestures and Cerise enters first. I follow her and Oosa says, "I will summon you once the guests have begun to arrive for the Queen's party. In the meanwhile, please rest well and enjoy our hospitality."

Oosa bows, exiting and the door slides closed behind us.

The room is similar to the one Sloan, Li, and Doran were taken to. There are two beds with elaborate, onyx-colored headboards and plush black bedspreads. The ceiling and walls are metal, but there are large, velvety purple panels displayed like artwork, which gives the room a little more warmth. Beneath the beds is another thick, silvery rug and above the beds hangs a chandelier identical to the one in the guys' room.

Opposite the door is a narrow window that runs from the floor all the way to the ceiling. Cerise walks over and stares out, the view of the tumultuous sea and the charcoal sky is unhindered. I come up beside her, the indigo crescent moon winking back at us.

"It's a weird place, isn't it?" Cerise asks.

"Eh, I've gotten used to weird," I reply leaning my shoulder against the glass so that I can stare out, but look at Cerise at the same time.

She's changed since being on Xon 9. Her pale skin still shines, but it's lost some of its opalescence. I wonder if being away from the sea will eventually make it disappear completely. Her hazel eyes still glow like little fires and are sharp and alert. Meanwhile, her body which was once curvaceous, has become more sinewy, her movements more precise. The jeweled handle of one of her daggers sparkles from its sheath on her hip, her black jacket pushed to the side.

"I guess…maybe just a little bit…I miss home." Her voice, usually assertive, is soft and hesitant. As if she's afraid to admit that she misses the place that tormented her heart.

"It's okay to miss it," I tell her. "It was all you ever knew. And it's okay to be afraid."

"These strange places. The redness of your home planet, and the darkness of this one. I never realized how bright and beautiful it all was, until I gave it all up." Her perfect pink mouth frowns.

"You don't regret your decision to come with us, do you?" Part of me doesn't want to know the answer to that. It was Cerise's sacrifice that allowed Sloan to survive and come home with me, which spared him a life as a cursed servant to the Water Queen. And another part of me knows that Cerise has the right to regret the decision she made those few months ago. Not that her regret could change the past, but maybe I could somehow make it up to her.

There's a long drawn out pause between us, but it's not uncomfortable. Somewhere in the hallway, soft, instrumental music is playing. For a moment, it drowns out the buzzing in my ears.

Finally, Cerise turns her eyes from the window. "No. No, I don't regret it. I'm scared, yes. And confused some of the time. But I have you and I have Li. Right now, that is enough." She turns back to the window, eyes focused on the crashing waves below. "It's more than I had when I left."

. . .

I'm sitting on a sandy beach, a blue sea crashing before me. The sky is cerulean and the sun hangs like a warm globe above me. I feel its heat on my cheeks and let out a breath I didn't even know that I'd been holding. I know that in actuality I'm sprawled out on a bed in Queen Isa's towers perched above the tumultuous sea, but it doesn't make this dream any less real.

My mother, being who she is, shares something in common with Sloan and Bina: the ability to communicate via dreams. I'm alone now, but I lean back on my elbows allowing them to sink into the soft sand, and wait. Birds sing and I can hear the faint sounds of insects. The high-pitched buzzing in my ears is gone, at least for now.

The waves lap at the toes of my boots. Before long I hear the gentle pad of bare feet down the stone pathway that leads from the castle to the pink sand. Tall blades of various beach grasses form a sort of natural wall between the castle and the shore. There's the soft swish of fabric as my mother sits down beside me.

As I suspected, she's barefoot, like every time I see her these days. She's wearing a sort of long, cotton dress with thin straps. It's sapphire blue and emphasizes her gray eyes. Her dark brown hair is swept up in a series of elaborate braids and she's wearing a crown made of tiny pink flowers. To anyone looking at us, we'd appear to be sisters—I'd obviously be the rebel, evil one with my sloppy ponytail, boots, and ragged sweater—and she would be the beautiful, good sister. But we're not sisters, of course. My mother has three forms: the maiden, the matron, and the krone. During her life on Xon 9—the life with my father and me—she was Novea, the matron.

But now, being banned from returning to the planet she loves so much, she has returned to the form of the maiden: Anuja. And although she looks younger, she has a few thousand years on me.

"You look happy," I say by way of greeting.

"As a clam," she smiles. Her voice hasn't changed, here it still rings like the loveliest of melodies. "And you look..." She frowns. "And just what is it that you look?"

I laugh, but it doesn't have much feeling behind it. "Tired? Scared? Like I just broke out of jail and was shot in the leg only a few days ago?"

"Hmmm. All of the above then. Shot! Oh my. That *is* serious." She purses her lips and under normal circumstances there would be some motherly lecture about who I hang out with, my choices, and how they affect my safety. But these aren't normal circumstances.

"It's fine. It was just in the thigh." I sound tougher than I feel. "How's dad?"

"He sends his well-wishes. He misses you."

"Why didn't he come then?" I absent-mindedly twirl the ring on my right index finger. The ring that would allow me to see him.

"It's too difficult for me. It's one thing for me to dream walk, but it's another to bring someone else along for the ride. Even my abilities have limitations." She's peering out at the sea—which is placid in comparison to the one outside the towers—and turns back to me. "Which is what I wanted to talk to you about."

"Dream walking?" That's one thing I have no interest in learning. As someone on the receiving end it's highly annoying to be pulled from your slumber at someone's beck and call.

"No, Kata. Limitations." Oh. You'd think with the whole living on different planets/universes/dimensions/whatever it is that you'd get lucky and be able to avoid certain things. Like the Parental Talk.

As if reading my mind she says, "Regardless of where you or I live—or what I look like—you're still my daughter. You're my responsibility and it's my job to ensure that you're prepared for what lies ahead of you."

"Yeah about that whole prepared thing."

"You were given your gifts for a reason. I know they may not all seem useful at the moment, but they will prove useful on your journey. Remember, not so much the gifts, but what the gifts stand for: Fire for courage and Earth for strength. Wood to see the whole of a situation. And Water to see the truth."

She continues. "That is the important thing, more important even than the gifts themselves." I want to reply, *Then why am I practically killing myself to get them?* But I don't because I've learned enough to know that sometimes I can't see the forest for the trees. "Remember that and you shall succeed in finding the Metal stone and returning safely home."

I want to ask so many things. Like, what does she know about the disease that is slowly spreading through the colony and that killed Ahna? Is Isa trustworthy? What if I can't do it? What if after all we've done, and all I've been through, in the end the Imminent Darkness still wins? What if everything I've ever loved is destroyed in the blink of an eye?

Instead, I say, "You said something about limitations."

"So I did," she smiles leaning her shoulder affectionately into mine. "Good to know you were listening. The physical manifestation of your gifts have limitations, but the true essence of your gifts can never be taken away. It's important that you remember that."

"True essence lasts forever. Got it."

Her smile fades and her face turns solemn. "I believe in you, Kata. So many people do. You only need to believe in and trust yourself. If you can do that, then you've already won because the Imminent Darkness doesn't even have that. Otherwise, it wouldn't need to do the things that it does in order to sustain itself."

I roll my eyes. "That was a corny Mom Talk."

She puts an arm around my shoulders, and pulls me into her chest, smashing my ear beneath her chin. "Well, you may have found it corny, but it's true." She releases me and sighs. "It's almost time. I think you have a party to attend?"

"Isa," I say as if that's all the answer she needs.

"Quite the character. Throwing a party as the world falls apart around her. Sounds about right." She gently grabs my chin so that I'm looking at her. It's an intimate gesture and although her face is no older than mine, her fathomless eyes show all of her years. "One more thing before you go. Okay, two. One, I love you."

The surrounding landscape begins to soften around her, like I am looking through a soft-focus lens. The dream is beginning to fade. I can feel someone shaking me awake and calling my name. The high-pitched buzzing is beginning to return.

"I love you too," I reply. "But what's the second thing?"

Her voice sounds far away when she replies. "Even the Imminent Darkness has limitations."

CHAPTER 12

We take the glass elevator up to the top level of the tallest tower. As we exit, it feels as though the ground is swaying beneath my feet and I'm glad that I don't have a fear of heights. Sloan nudges my arm and points upward. The roof of the tallest tower has peeled back leaving an unhindered view of the dark smoke-colored sky and slice of purple moon. Silver pinpricks glow down on us, blanketing everything in shimmery soft light.

The party's already in full swing. There are people—and creatures—everywhere, bodies squished together. Music pulsates from two massive speakers that flank a floating table where a man who looks similar to Oosa, but with rainbow-colored cracks of lightning instead of white ones, and wearing neon-colored sunglasses, stands. He has a pair of headphones slung around his black neck and he's messing with a set of controls on top of the table.

Everyone seems exceptionally tall in this Land. There are more beings who look like Oosa and like the music spinner. I remember Isa had called them Fulgurs. The music spinner's obsidian skin flashes in a brilliant streak of turquoise. Anyone human-like looks similar to Isa. Tall and thin with pale skin. Everyone's clothes are dark and tight. I feel undressed in my jeans, t-shirt, and oversized sweater

A lithe woman dances on top of some sort of large, marble column. She has on a black leather mini-dress and her dark brown hair is cut short and spiky with purple tips. Her boots go up to the middle of her thighs and her dress is so short it leaves little to the imagination.

Doran's jaw drops as his brown eyes fall on her. The woman comes out of her trancelike dancing and notices him staring. She winks and I notice that her eyelashes are long and silver. Taking in the room, there are several more columns with women and men dancing on top of them. Bodies coalesce across the black marble floor, throwing themselves into one another beneath the mysterious sky. There are periodic flashes of colorful light, emitting from the music spinner's body and they light up the crowd in various shades of orange, yellow, green, and blue.

To my right, a man dressed in a tuxedo, with tails trailing all the way to the floor and complete with a top hat, spins a ball of crackling light in the palm of his hand. The woman who Doran had been staring at on the column catches his attention with a loud whistle and he tosses the ball of light toward her. She dips backwards, arching her back in a way that seems like a violation of physics, but she catches it and when she does her entire body is cast in a brilliant white glow as the ball of light seems to unravel and spin around her like an extra-long piece of ribbon. It doesn't seem to faze her though as she continues to rock her body back and forth in time to the music.

Sloan takes my hand and leads me through the crowd. The music is so loud I can feel the bass through the soles of my feet. In the crowd to our left is another man in a tuxedo juggling several balls of light. They move so fast, they're nothing but a continuous circle of light. I bump into several people, their bodies dewy with sweat. People are dancing, kissing, careening all around us. The random colors of bright light bounce off their faces until, like the juggler's balls, all I can see is a continuous blur of rainbow in the sea of people around us.

Somewhere behind me, Li, Cerise, and Doran have faded away, swallowed up by the crowd. The music has replaced the high-pitched buzzing in my ears, but I can feel it moving through my entire body. The energy of the crowd is frenetic and chaotic. Sloan leads me to the other side of the room where there's a balcony that juts out and over the jagged rocks we couldn't cross earlier. The sea is a darker shade of gray, bursting into foamy white as it crashes against the base of the mountains. From up here, the sea looks like it could go on forever. Except I know that it doesn't because Isa told me it would lead us to the Isle of the Tonitrui.

Sloan places a hand on the small of my back, a warm reassurance that is like a pool of calm from the frenzied energy of the party. I wonder if he is missing what was lost to him. If he can sense the absence of the Water's presence as acutely as I can sense the absence of the fifth Element in my blood. An emptiness that rushes through me and loops around my heart, despite the other four rushing to try and fill it; it is an unfillable space.

He leans down and whispers in my ear. "You're right." I close my eyes and open them again. I forget sometimes that he can do that. For the most part, he doesn't read my mind—another one of his many talents—but sometimes in intimate moments I think that he almost can't help it. I let my vulnerability slide and my thoughts unwittingly slip into his. I turn into him so that we are chest to chest. His heartbeat nearly matched to mine, strong and steady despite the pulsating music around us. In the sea of chaos, he is my calm.

"Don't say it," he says softly, his voice breaking slightly on the last word. I want to say that I'm sorry, sorry a thousand times over for what loving me has done to him—and what it will do to him. What it will do to me when I go on living and he lives only the span of a mortal life. I want to apologize for what's been done, but I also want to apologize for what's yet to come.

But I don't. Instead I hold both of his now-smooth cheeks in my rough hands, and pull his face down toward mine, our lips finding each other easily. His hand is still on the small of my back and he pulls me in closer. I can smell the sweat from the crowd of people mixed with the scent of his shower soap. And I wish that it all could just end here. That this was the end of the journey, but it's only the beginning.

As if in answer to my thoughts, the crowd grows silent. The music softens to a quiet, steady pulse. We pull away from one another, but Sloan's hand still remains wrapped around mine. The music spinner speaks into an amplifier: "Presenting Queen Isa, third daughter of the Universe, and ruler of Terra Metalli."

The energy of the room has changed slightly and from our position on the outskirts, we watch as the crowd parts in the center and forms a ring around an open area. There's a rumble in the floor and for a moment I think that the music spinner has restarted the music, but it's the sound of the floor opening and a large pedestal rising from the darkness below. A great, metal column that glimmers in the starlight and reflects the Fulgurs' rainbow of colors.

Atop the pedestal, draped coyly across a purple, velvet couch with an ornate, onyx colored frame is Isa. Her long, black hair is done up in elaborate twists and is adorned with the same silver, star luminescence as the chandeliers and sconces. She holds her scepter in one hand and it crackles with the same frenetic energy as the party only moments before, and I wonder if somehow Isa controls the energy not only of the land, but of her people. When the pedestal stops moving, Isa rises from the couch. Her dress is tight purple leather, and like the other woman, leaves little to the imagination, with its short length and plunging neckline, but the way in which she wears it—or rather commands that *it* wear her—makes the other woman look like a school-girl. I wish I could see Doran's face, but he's lost somewhere in the throng of people.

Isa's voice booms out over the enthusiastic crows of her people, loud and with a sharp edge that ripples out and over the same as the music spinner's songs. "Citizens of the fair Terra Metalli, we celebrate tonight the arrival of my niece and her friends." She points the scepter at me and immediately I'm awash in a glow of silvery light. I don't know what I should do. Do I wave? Bow? Curtsey? But, lucky for me, Isa spares me the decision by continuing her speech.

"Soon, she will be embarking on a challenging journey and her success will be detrimental to the life of our own humble land." I look around at the people, in their sexy clothing, and elaborate light tricks and think that humble in the Land of Metal looks quite a bit different than humble on Xon 9. "So, my people, tonight we will party harder than we ever have before. Tonight we party as if it is our last!" Her voice crescendos at the end into a booming note of finality, and despite the somewhat macabre message the crowd breaks out into applause and cheering, jumping up and down as the music spinner restarts the music and once again the silence is lost to the sound of throbbing bass and crackling energy.

. . .

Somehow I have the feeling that at every party Isa throws, they party 'like it's their last'. More light magicians appear, performing tricks with the balls of light much to the amusement of the party-goers. The music thumps a pounding bass, drowning out the thunder that would normally crack at regular intervals. White lightning slashes across the charcoal sky above the heads of the crowd, but no one seems to notice. People jerk and sway to the music, throwing themselves into one another in a tangle of arms and legs.

Sloan takes my hand and leads me from the balcony and back into the melee, but I immediately feel his hand slip from mine as I'm caught up in a rush of people, sweaty bodies crushing against me from either side. I call his name, but the word is immediately swallowed up by the crowd of people. A man brushes against my shoulder and turns to apologize. His eyes seem to glow in the lack of light, beautiful colors dancing off his angular face. His pale blonde hair is in a short ponytail with shaved sides.

"Want to amp up your party, Princess?" he asks and holds out a thin-fingered hand. Something small glows blue-white in his palm. He grins at me and his mouth is lit up the same color as the weird thing in his hand.

Suddenly, Li is behind me and pushing me out of the way. "She's not interested in your Insanis." He says in a low growl. His grip is tight on my shoulder as he steers me away from the center of the crowd and toward the sides where the crowd is thinner, but where some women and men are dancing on top of the tall marble columns.

"Insanis?" I ask.

Li nods, leaning in close to my ear to be heard over the music spinner's beats. "It's a hallucinogen."

I scowl. "I don't want to know how you know."

"I know a lot of things." Li shrugs.

"But we're practically in a different world!" I protest.

"And yet some things still stay the same. A party can't just be a good time. When you party as often as these people do, the natural high begins to fade. So they amp it up with drugs." It sounds like something that would be available back home in the Black Bazaar. I want to ask if he knows because he's tried it, but I don't think I want to know the answer to that. Li can have his secrets and I'll have mine.

His hand slides from my shoulder down to my hand and he leads me toward a small cluster of black chairs where Cerise and Doran are waiting. Cerise's face is shell-shocked to say the least. I don't think the Land of Water had entertainment quite like this. An extraordinarily tall girl, who appears about our age, but who can be sure in a place like this, is leaned over Doran's shoulder, long dark hair spilling into his lap. She's whispering in his ear, and his eyes are wide. Doran is from the Underground and his sister works in the Black Bazaar at a tattoo parlor. If Li's seen parties like this before, then I'm sure Doran has as well. The girl gives him an imploring look and his eyes dart to mine. I shrug. Who am I to stop his good time, after all the party is in our honor. He shoots me a thankful grin and the girl smiles, grabbing his arm and leading him into the crowd of people. They're swallowed up in seconds.

Cerise leans over to me. "Are parties always like this?"

Li leans into her, his voice low but still audible over the thumping bass. "Only the best ones," he grins. A rosy flush creeps across Cerise's pale skin, visible even in the dim light. "Wanna try out those land-legs with a dance?" he asks, taking her hand in his.

Cerise grins, and it lights up her entire face. Her red hair is in loose waves that tumble to her shoulders and in appearance alone she looks as if she could belong in this peculiar place, even more so than the rest of us. "Why not?"

Li practically beams as he bows slightly. Cerise stands and even in her t-shirt and jeans she looks as elegant as any of the leather-clad dancers that twirl and sway around the room. He twirls her and pulls her into him, leading her out into the crush of people, heads touching in a way that's so intimate it surprises me. There had been a time when I thought I would date Li, but I think deep down I knew that despite surface appearances, we were too much alike. Both craving the same things, both looking for something outside of ourselves, when what we needed wasn't out there to be found. A love between us would have consumed us both until nothing was left but dying embers. A love like that could have been beautiful. But it would have been dangerous.

I startle out of my thoughts as someone sits down next to me.

It's Isa.

"Sorry to startle you, Little Niece. Your friends are having a good time?" She's languidly draped across the chair beside me, legs crossed demurely revealing miles of pale skin. She twirls her scepter in between her fingers like a baton. I look back toward the crowd, scanning for signs of Sloan—his mop of shaggy brown hair, or a glimmer of sea green eyes. But I don't see him.

I turn back to Isa, whose own black eyes are locked on me as if she's studying me, sizing me up for the task at hand. She doesn't frighten me like Tullia. At least not yet.

"It's…interesting," I reply honestly.

She smiles, and her mouth is lit up like the man with the Insanis.

Her teeth glow a blue-white, but unlike the man it doesn't reach her eyes. White lightning flashes in them and she blinks ridiculously long purple eyelashes as if she can blink away the fact that her freaking eyeballs have electricity in them. Energy cackles around us. The sound of the party fades away. I can still see it, and still hear it, but it seems far away.

"That's better. These things get so dreadfully loud. They're a boisterous bunch, the citizens of the towers."

"They all live here?" I ask, realizing she's somehow manipulated the energy of the room to give us a quiet bubble of space despite the goings-on around us.

"More or less. There's not much inhabitable land here. Just the towers and the Isle of the Tonitrui." She smiles. "Until we figure out how to build cities on the sea. Or in the sky."

That would definitely be a sight to see and somehow I don't doubt that if Isa wanted it, it would happen.

"Do you always throw parties like this?" I ask scanning the crowd again for Sloan's familiar shape and coming up empty.

"Often enough, but none this lavish, except for special occasions." Isa's voice is slow and even.

"Except this isn't just an ordinary special occasion," I say turning back toward her.

"Indeed, your arrival, dear Niece, is of the most special variety."

But I know my mother and her sisters better than they think I do. I know that they do nothing, without something being in it for them.

"But there's more. We journey tomorrow. We should be resting. But you decided to throw us a party. Why?" Ever since we've arrived my brain has seemed to be moving in slow motion. But now in this space of calm that Isa has cultivated, the bass a dull thump and the buzzing in my ears gone momentarily, I feel like I can finally think again, unhindered by the strange energy of this Land.

"You're smarter than I give you credit for, Daughter of Anuja. I wanted to show you my people. How happy they are, how carefree." She gestures at the crowd that's still a chaotic frenzy of limbs and heads bobbing to the music. "I want you to see what is at stake if you fail."

I feel my stomach clench. "I already know what is at stake, Aunt Isa." I reply through clenched teeth. "I have seen my mother almost killed, my father kidnapped, and my friends die. I think I understand more than anybody what is at stake here."

Quick as lightning, Isa is leaned over, her beautiful face only inches from mine. Her breath is sweet and flowery as she says softly, "But do you?" She pulls away, stands up and begins to pace. Her stilettos click with each step. "Your little planet is not the only one affected. We are all affected by the Imminent Darkness. My people do not see it, do not feel it. But I do. I know it is there and I know it is waiting. I protect them the best that I can, throw lavish parties to distract them when I need to. But I can't protect them forever." Her voice takes on a strange, winsome tone. Despite her moodiness, Isa truly cares for her people. She stares off into the crowd of people and I feel a surge of bass as the energetic shield begins to fade. "Forever is a long time to be alone." Her last word is swallowed up by boisterous voices and the resurgence of the music.

Suddenly, I feel very confused and very tired as if all the energy has been drained from my body. I yawn, too tired to get up and search for Sloan in the crowd. But I don't have to. He appears out of nowhere.

"There you are," he says. He takes my hand and pulls me to my feet. "You look exhausted. Let's get you out of here."

"The others?" I ask, stifling another yawn unable to battle this sudden weariness that has been seemingly thrust on to me.

"They'll be fine. I think Doran's having the time of his life. Anyway, they'll pay for it in the morning probably, but for now let them enjoy it while they can." He doesn't have to say because who knows what will happen? Who knows how much longer we all have to be carefree and just have fun like normal young adults do? As we walk hand in hand back toward the elevators, the unspoken questions loom heavy on my shoulders. As the elevator doors slide closed, they're still waiting for an answer.

CHAPTER 13

Sloan and I are already at the long table in the dining hall. We sit clustered at one end, the rest of the table empty. Isa isn't joining us, I guess, and Oosa brought us a breakfast of something rubbery and something else hard as stone. I poke my fork at it. The water tastes okay. It's hard to mess up water, right?

I look up as Cerise, Doran, and Li enter the dining hall. Or rather, more like stumble into the dining hall. Doran takes one look at the questionable plate of food sitting at his table place and looks like he's going to be sick.

Cerise looks as though she ran a marathon. Her eyes are tired and her hair is in a sloppy ponytail, instead of its usual braid. Li on the other hand looks chipper as all get out. I can't say that I'm surprised. This is the Liwald Sollomon life style.

He plops down in the empty chair at the head of the table and picks up the unidentifiable rubbery object and takes a big bite. He chews at it for a while with a weird look on his face before swallowing. Nodding, he says, "Not bad."

I think that Doran's skin actually turns a visible shade of green.

Oosa returns to the table with three additional glasses of water and sets them down. "When you're ready, Miss, your ship is all set for departure. The Navigation System coordinates to the Isle of Tonitrui have been programmed." He bows slightly.

"Thank you, Oosa. I think we'll just be another few moments. Is Aunt Isa not coming down to see us off?" I ask, placing my fork beside my plate, my food remaining untouched. My messenger bag has a bottle of nutrient pills from the tent city, along with a thermos of water. It will just have to do for now.

"The queen has a headache this morning, but she wishes you and your friends safe travels to the Isle of Tonitrui. She hopes that you fare well and have a speedy return." He bows again and disappears through a doorway, his skin flashing in a cacophony of white light.

"A headache," Li scoffs once Oosa is out of earshot. Even he isn't dumb enough to criticize the queen in front of her most loyal servant. "More like an Insanis hangover. She's lucky if a headache is all she ends up with."

"What does it do to you?" Sloan asks poking at the stone-like thing on his plate and then giving up and taking a drink of water instead.

Li smiles, happy to enlighten us of the effects of all things hallucinatory and illegal. Well, illegal at home. "Insanis, in its pure form, affects receptors in your brain's cortex. It disrupts your body's serotonin." This is the most intellectual I've ever heard Li sound and I think for a moment it's too bad that he goofed around in school so often. A glance across the table reveals that Sloan is thinking the exact same thing.

Doran waves his hand. "In English, please."

"It makes you feel good. But in a synthetic kind of way that alters the brain's communication style. Really, the affects depend on how often the drug is used and for how long. Isa raved pretty hard, and it sounds like these parties are a fairly regular occurrence. I'd say she's still feeling some of the after-shocks. Nausea, dehydration, a tingling of the skin."

Cerise eyes Li suspiciously. "And just how do you know so much about it?"

He slings an arm over the back of her chair. "Babe. That was a different life. I'm a changed man." This makes me even more thankful that I haven't told Li about that little immortal thing he's got going on.

"Why would Isa let something like that be used at her parties?" I wonder out loud.

"Dunno. Maybe it drowns out that star-forsaken buzzing sound," Doran says and shakes his head as if he can clear it of cobwebs.

"The energy here is definitely strange," Sloan comments. "It's chaotic and…electric."

"Literally," Cerise says downing her glass of water. "You saw those light magicians with their balls of light."

"It kind of reminds me of home. The way the planet seems to affect their physiology," Sloan taps his fingers on the table, as if his mind is on other things. I can already see the wheels beginning to turn, analyzing the situation, comparing these people in the Land of Metal to the ones whom he grew up with.

"Except, it affects their energy more than anything. Maybe something like Insanis can calm it down. Chill them out," Li says.

"Maybe. But I think it's more than that."

I follow Sloan's eyes to the far wall, which is lined with several large windows. Outside, the sky is the same charcoal gray as the day before and the silver starlight still glows softly. But instead of the indigo moon, which has turned a pale lavender color against the sky, a brilliant sun bathes the planet in blood-red. At home, the sun is red and never sets, but the effect isn't quite as harsh as it is here. At night the light of the twin moons coats everything in a soft pink. But here the sun hangs close and large. The window panes glow like bloody pools on the floor.

. . .

We follow Oosa back to the hangar on the basement floor. When we reach the sliding door, we're joined by another man identical in appearance to Oosa, but named Aama. I wonder how Isa—or anyone for that matter—can tell them apart. Oosa tells us we are in good hands with Aama and wishes us a safe journey, before disappearing to tend to his queen.

Aama is a bit less talkative than Oosa. His lithe form glows with

entire 2.3 tetras?"

"Not necessary," Aama explains. "The ship only needs sentient steering during take-off and landing. Otherwise, it is programmed to an autopilot interface." He pauses briefly and Sloan nods in understanding and I'm glad at least one person understands what's going on. And I'm extra glad that for once it isn't me. It's nice to be able to share the responsibility for once. "Is there anything else for which I can do for you before your departure?"

"No, Aama. I think that will be all. We truly appreciate all you've done to help us," Sloan says running a hand lightly over the lit up dashboard controls. I notice a slight smile on his face and realize that he's actually *excited* for this journey.

Aama bows. "I wish you a speedy return and a journey unhindered by difficulty." He disappears down the ship's ramp, and it rises up with a hiss then locks into place, effectively sealing us in. I only realize after he's gone, his peculiar choice of words.

. . .

"Well, this is lovely," Li comments as he settles into one of the black cushioned benches. Sloan's exit of the hangar went smoothly, much to everyone's surprise. Including his own. The ship has begun to play some sort of instrumental music through its speakers.

I stand beside him at the dashboard of controls, peering out the narrow windshield. His hands move easily over the different knobs and controls, guiding us low over the jagged rocks that surround the towers. Everything is cast in a tint of blood-red and the sun hangs so close to the horizon it looks as if it could just drop into the sea at any moment. White lightning still cracks in the sky above us, creating jagged lines that flash then fade. Sloan begins an ascent and I grip the dashboard as we soar upward, picking up speed. We have to navigate through a narrow pass between the mountains in order to get to the open sky above the sea.

Sloan's hands loosely grip two levers, moving them slowly back and forth. It's only another moment before the mountains loom in front of us, gray and foreboding. The small ship seems unfazed by the wind that whips off the mountain peaks. I glance at the map and see the narrow pass that leads to the open sky above the turbulent sea. When I look back up, two mountains loom in front of us. A narrow pass appears like a crack in the wall of rock. Sloan moves his hand to a flat, square space on the dashboard, that's lit from the inside and glows a soft green. He moves his fingers softly to the right and the entire ship tilts slowly to the right.

"You might want to hold on," he says, never taking his eyes off the peak of sky that appears between the two mountains. I grip the dashboard and hear Cerise let out a cry as we continue to angle to the right. The pass grows from a crack to a larger crevice that looks barely large enough to fit the ship. Sloan increases the angle and I close my eyes, reopening them at the last second.

We rush through the pass and out into the open air, and I imagine a butterfly emerging from a cocoon. A small opening that grows larger, until the butterfly can burst out and soar into the open air. Nothing lies in front of us. There are no man-made structures and no buildings to obstruct our view. Sloan's fingers slide across the pad again, this time to the left, righting the ship so that we're flying parallel to the sea below.

"Well, that was something," he breathes softly and his green eyes are wild and happy. He's wearing an expression I've never seen before.

"Thanks for the warning, Captain. Are there even seatbelts on these things?" Li grumbles. Cerise is now standing behind my shoulder and she points out the windshield.

"It reminds me of home. Well, except for the gigantic sun part. But the endless water. I wouldn't have thought a place like this…so far away…could remind me of something so familiar." Her voice is tinged with sadness. But she shakes her head and pats Sloan on the shoulder. "I think you did a wonderful job, Sloan."

He grins, but doesn't take his eyes off the dashboard.

"I'm hungry. Come find these so-called provisions with me, Cerise?" Li asks from behind us.

"I think I'll help," Doran pipes up, still strangely quiet since last night's party.

"Good luck with that," I say as the three of them disappear into one of the many hallways that lead away from the ship's center and toward its back and sides.

According to Aama, the ship's interior is a ring with a semi-circle at the back. The front of the ring is the cockpit and off the cockpit are several hallways, like spokes, that lead to the back parts of the ship where bunks, a small kitchen, a toilet and storage room are located.

Sloan continues to fly the ship parallel to the sea, nothing but charcoal and scarlet sky above us. He hits some buttons on the control panel and the instrumental music stops and a mechanical voice that sounds oddly like Oosa says, "Auto-control Pilot engaged." Only then does Sloan remove his hands from the dashboard and let them fall loosely to his sides.

I put an arm around his waist. "That was amazing. I didn't know you could fly a ship."

He laughs. "Me neither." He looks down at me and his eyes are still alight with what I now realize is a combination of wonder and joy.

"Well, you'd never have guessed that Aama just explained everything to you a little bit ago." I lean my head on his shoulder. "It's weird isn't it?" Looking out at the sea as we fly above it has an almost dizzying effect, so I move my eyes up and to the horizon.

Sloan takes my hand, entwining his fingers with mine and pulls me toward the circle of seats in the recessed area of the cockpit. From this angle, we can only see the sky through the windshield, the rest of the view cut off from us.

He rubs his thumb back and forth over the back of my hand. Secretly, I enjoy these moments of calm, when just for a few moments I can feel normal. Like I'm not destined to save the Universe or defeat an ancient, dark force. That I'm just me and Sloan is just him, and that's all that there is. All that matters.

"It's not so weird," he finally says. The instrumental music has turned back on and I feel like we're on some kind of vacation as opposed to a dangerous mission. "I used to have this dream, when I was a kid." He stops abruptly and looks down at me. From this angle, my head near his shoulder looking up, I can see the smooth angles of his face and my eyes know exactly where the gills used to be in his neck, the only reminder that anything was ever there, a pale, thin scar on either side of his Adam's apple. He has stubble on his chin and a crease between his brows. I don't remember the crease being there before.

He continues. "I used to have this dream that I could fly. In it, I would open my bedroom window in our little trailer and slip out into the pink night. And I would just float above the people of the Black Bazaar. I would soar higher and higher, so high that I could see the mountains past the periphery. The twin moons would shine above me and I'd call out to the never-setting sun. Below me the houses of the colony, the University Complex, Council Hall, all of it would just be tiny, little specks. Like nothing at all. Of course, that's not true. Everything that mattered to me." He looks down at me. "And even the stuff I didn't yet know mattered to me, was down there. But I felt so…free. It was just me and the sky. There was no separation. Those dreams were my favorite."

There's a long pause before I ask, "Do you still have them?"

He shakes his head, nuzzling his chin into my hair. "No. It's been years. Eventually, they stopped. When Finn was taken away. That's when I stopped having them." I close my eyes and listen to the steady beat of his heart. Strong and reassuring. How fast did he have to grow up after Finn was arrested? He was the only man in the house after that, did he feel it was his responsibility then to take care of Bina and Michaela? And now, here I was asking him to take care of and protect me. But who is it that's protecting and taking care of him?

"Finn's back now," I say softly and I know it isn't enough. "And you got to fly. For real. Isn't it a strange coincidence that your dream stopped when Finn was gone, but then your dream sort of comes true when he returns?" Am I grasping at straws? I don't know, but it seems peculiar on a bigger scale, like looking out the narrow windshield of the ship. From down here I can only see the red-gray sky, but if I stand up I can see the sea and the horizon. I can't shake the feeling that we're only seeing part of the bigger picture.

"My dream has already come true," he says pulling his face away so he can look down at me. I feel my cheeks grow warm. The memory of the time Sloan first came to me in my dreams, before my Pronouncement, rushes back to me. I had no idea then. No idea who he was or who I was. I remember the mixed emotions I felt at seeing him in such an intimate way. I remember I woke up and my pillow was wet, as if it had been plucked from the sea and placed on my bed. That was when Sloan was still a Water.

But is he still? Are we still our Elemental if it has been drained from our entire being? Is Li still a Fire? I feel like it can't be as simple as that. Despite, his Water being gone, Sloan is still the same person. He is still my anchor to what's real. My reminder of all I have to lose, but also of all I have to gain.

I know it's corny, but I reply anyways, "Mine too." His lips find mine and I can feel the truth of the words confirmed between us.

CHAPTER 14

I lean on the dashboard and peer out the windshield. The night passed uneventfully. And the provisions Aama stocked for us left a lot to be desired, but it was better than nothing. The ship is still flying itself on autopilot. Soft instrumental music fills the cockpit. I'm the only one awake because I couldn't sleep.

The indigo moon is a faded thumbnail in the sky and the charcoal sky is lit blood red at the horizon, reflecting in the sea like an open wound. Inside the ship I can no longer feel the land's peculiar energy and the buzzing in my ears has ceased, at least for now.

The sun heaves itself above the horizon and immediately bathes everything in a brilliant red light. It climbs up the gray sky until it pauses part way as if to take a rest. According to the navigation, we're heading north.

Even though this place is so different from home, the prime reason being the surplus of surface water which is severely lacking on Xon 9. At home, water is pumped up through a complex network of drills and wells. But the brilliant red sun reflecting over the landscape is familiar and my eyes adjust easily. Lightning flashes in the east followed by a muffled clash of thunder.

I try to remember what Isa told me about the Tonitrui. She had said they were brave, but also that they were cunning. She'd said the Chief Tonitrui would know how we could find the Metal stone, but that he would expect something in return. Well, Li can definitely be cunning. I can't count how many times since we were kids that he'd misconstrue my words. So at least we could be even there, if the Chief tries to get tricky with us. And Doran is one of the bravest people, I've ever met. Sloan is too, but he has an even better advantage because of his family. He grew up—like Doran—around Metals, but unlike Doran, he grew up around Metals with unique abilities. What the rest of the colony would call Unbalanced Metals. Although, I now know Bina and Finn are both far from it. *Hmpf.* If anyone's Unbalanced, it's Michaela the Vigilante.

Then there's Cerise. Also, incredibly brave, but also fierce with a dagger or a bow and arrow. She's a quick and clean fighter. She laid me out numerous times when we trained together. I rub my shoulder where I took a particularly bad hit; it still aches from time to time despite the days that have passed. Even more noteworthy, is that out of all of us she probably has the least to lose. And that can make a person do things they wouldn't ever normally do.

164

I stare at the dizzying sea rushing beneath the ship a moment longer, before pushing myself away and back toward the seated area. My messenger bag was tossed onto one of the seats the previous day and now I open it, fishing inside for a small burlap sack. My fingers find it and I pull it out. At one time it contained four items: a speckled feather, a pack of matches from a place called The Tavern and the Sea, a vial of clear liquid that turned out to be some kind of acid, and a small crystal. Now, all that's left is the crystal. I pull it out and flip onto my back, resting my head on top of my messenger bag like a pillow. The light's fairly dim in the cabin, but I hold up the crystal anyways, peering at it with one eye-closed. It's multi-faceted and so clear that if I wave my fingers on the other side I can see them. Rainbows dance on the other side of the prism. The crystal is cool to the touch.

"How will you destroy a stone?" I ask it. Small, but strong. Perhaps, it holds secrets of its own. The instrumental music still plays softly and I can feel my eyelids finally growing heavy with the sleep that wouldn't come to me the night before. My arm slips to rest across my chest, the crystal still between my fingers.

Even though my body is tired, my brain still reels with thoughts from the first time I met Bina and from the second time when she gave me the small burlap sack that would help me destroy the stones. I can still remember the milky white of her eyes as she told me that I was all possibilities and yet I was none, the way her cold, bony fingers gripped my wrist like iron, even as I tried to twist away.

Memories—not originally mine—mix in: Bina being given the

stones for safe-keeping, then informing my mom to get rid of them in order to protect me. Her cracked voice reciting the ominous prophecy that when I no longer need protecting, the world as we know it will cease to exist. My brain begins to get fuzzy around the edges and I can feel my thoughts tumbling around on top of one another.

What will happen to Sloan when I no longer need protecting? To us? What do those strange words even mean? I'm suddenly too tired to sort it out and my eyelids slip closed, my other arm sliding down so that my knuckles hit the floor, and I fall into a fitful sleep.

. . .

I'm standing on a desolate landscape. The ground is dry and laced with fissures, as if it's shriveled up from lack of hydration. I look up. The sky above me is blood red. One sun, no moons. I push the sleeves up on my long-sleeved t-shirt. There's no breeze and the air is hot and humid, pressing in from all sides like a thick blanket. I turn in a slow circle, scanning through the haze. I've had these dreams before and I have a pretty good feeling of whose coming. And it's been too long since she's paid me a visit.

A small, shrunken figure wearing a long hooded cloak approaches. I immediately recognize the slow, careful steps. But I know that she is stubborn and doesn't take kindly to either help or pity. I wait patiently until her shuffled steps reach me and she lowers the hood.

"Bina," I say softly and step forward to close the distance between us and embrace her in a hug. She looks better than the last time I'd seen her in person—at Michaela's. Her hair is still a wild, grayed halo around her head, but her gray eyes are sharper and more alert. In my embrace, she feels more solid and less fragile. The MindCleanse the so-called Citizen Law Enforcement tried to conduct on her some months ago nearly killed her. But it isn't so easy to wipe away the memories of a Seer.

"Tis good to see yeh, Girl," Bina says pulling back from the hug and inspecting me shrewdly "But we don't have much time."

"Is everything okay? Is the tent city still safe?" I ask immediately.

"Yes. Yes. Everything is as it was when ye left. But it's yer adventure in the Land of Metal that I came to discuss."

"It's a strange place," I note. But it seems a little silly considering we're standing in some sort of wasteland.

"The Land of Metal has many secrets just like its inhabitants. Ye need to learn those secrets."

"How do you learn someone's secrets? Isn't that why they're called secrets? Because they aren't easy to find out?" I pick at my fingernail. Sometimes talking to Bina is like running in circles.

"No one said it would be easy. But learn someone's secrets and ye hold their power." Her words ring both familiar and true.

"How? These people—these creatures—are unlike any I've ever seen before. They're all…" My voice trails off. I was going to say they're all energy, but we're all made up of energy. The entire Universe is energy.

"Yes, they are different, but they all have a beating heart the same as yeh or me." She thinks about it for a second. "More or less. The point is yeh need to get them to trust yeh. Yeh were told of the Tonitrui?" I nod. "They especially. They can be tricksters, but if ye prove ye are as cunning as they, then they will respect yeh. Respect leads to trust. Learn their secrets and use them wisely."

Bina always has a habit of being super cryptic, and apparently today is no exception.

"Got it. Be cunning, but not too cunning. Get the Tonitrui to respect me and once they respect me, they'll trust me, thus laying bare all their soul's secrets."

Bina laughs. "Don't be silly, Girl. The Tonitrui don't have souls."

Greeeeaaat. As if being deceptive and cunning wasn't enough, now they're also apparently lacking in a little thing called a soul. Just when I thought things were beginning to look up. Or not.

As if reading my mind, Bina's face grows solemn once again. "Yeh, can do it, Impossible Girl. Ka."

She glances over her shoulder as if she is seeing something that I cannot. Dry, red land and blood red sky is all that looks back at me. I always wondered how the dream walking worked from the other side. Do they go into some sort of trance? Just look like they're sleeping as they travel across time and space into other people's sleep consciousness?

"Just remember what I told yeh. Oh, and don't forget." She begins to go fuzzy around the edges, much like the memories before I fell asleep and I recognize that the dream is beginning to fade. "They need to respect and trust yeh, but not the other way around."

Before I can ask for clarification she begins to fade, like the indigo moon during sunrise.

. . .

The cobwebs of my dream visit with Bina still linger in my mind. Stuff about secrets and power, and something about getting the Chief Tonitrui to trust me. Although, one part stands out. I distinctly remember Bina telling me that the Tonitrui don't have souls. And, back to that whole being honest thing I've been working on, it kind of scares the crap out of me that they supposedly don't have souls. Because if you don't have a soul, then what have you got to lose?

I'm beginning to feel like my time in the Land of Metal is more than just about getting the Metal stone. The stone must be found and it must be destroyed, but I can't shake the feeling that I'm supposed to be paying closer attention while I'm here. Like there could be a pop quiz later.

Doran pushes my legs off the cushioned bench and sits down beside me. He's noisily eating something. Seeing my expression, he holds it out to me. It's rectangular, white, and kind of resembles a sponge. "Want some?"

My stomach turns. "Uh, no thanks. I'll pass." I scoot back so that I'm sitting up and pull my messenger bag into my lap.

Cerise sits down on my other side. "I've been having the strangest dreams since we've been here."

"Really?" Doran asks through a mouthful of whatever it is that he's eating.

"I wouldn't say they're nightmares exactly. Just peculiar." She looks over her shoulder where Li and Sloan are deep in conversation as they enter from the back of the ship. Sloan is gesticulating adamantly and Li looks disinterested. I suppose some things never change.

Cerise continues, her voice lowered. "Dreams about Li."

"Is this something you should be sharing?" Doran asks, he wipes a white flake from his upper lip.

Cerise cuts him a withering glare. "Not those kinds of dreams. Strange ones. Involving the Tonitrui and the Fulgurs. I have a bad feeling about it. I don't think Isa is telling us the whole truth."

"What do you mean?" I ask. The hair on the back of my neck has begun to stand on end, my telltale sign for something bad about to happen.

"I think that the Fulgurs and the Tonitrui don't get along. And I think that Isa has offered refuge to the Fulgurs, in exchange for their servitude, and that it doesn't make the Tonitrui very happy."

"So she's sending us into a warzone?" Doran asks, cutting to the point.

Cerise shrugs. "I don't know. They're just dreams after all."

"Dreams can mean more than you realize," I reply. "We shouldn't ignore it. But what does Li have to do with anything?"

Cerise bites her bottom lip. "That's just it. In my dream, there's a battle and during the battle Li dies. He's killed right in front of me. Only," she hesitates as if considering whether to tell us the rest. But she's already gone this far. "He lives. I watch him die, over and over again, and each time he gets up or opens his eyes. And just like that, he's alive again." She chuckles a little. "Weird, right?"

I let out a too-loud laugh. "Yeah, that's pretty weird." *Get a grip.*

"A battle, huh?" Doran considers this. "I did overhear someone at the party refer to the Tonitrui as barbarians. That can't be good, can it?"

I worry the loose threads on the strap of my bag. "Isa told me they can be cunning. Tricksters. But she didn't say anything about them being enemies."

Cerise looks worried. "Sometimes it isn't so much what someone says as what they don't say."

At that Sloan and Li finally join us, Sloan standing behind me and placing a hand on either of my shoulders, like a comforting weight.

"We should arrive in 1.5 tetras according to the NS. I think that we should have some sort of plan for when we arrive," Sloan says, absent-mindedly rubbing my shoulders.

"Do they even know that we're coming?" Li asks. He sits on the other side of the benches, as if it's us versus him. Of course it's not like that at all. But I can't help but think of how he's not like the rest of us, and yet he doesn't even know it yet. The immortal and the (mostly) mortals.

"I have no idea. Isa didn't say. She just told me that they would be able to help me find the Metal stone."

"How convenient that the queen has seemed to have left out some important details." Li kicks his boots up onto the meal table in the center of the circle. "Perhaps, the timing of her party was more than just a party. Maybe it was a way to avoid having us ask questions that she didn't want to answer."

"Either way, it doesn't change anything," I point out. "I'm not sure how much Isa knows. And even if she's using us, we still need to find the stone."

"I just hope she isn't sending us on a wild goose chase." Li looks down at this lap. "We're running out of time."

For only a moment, I feel selfish for bringing him. But he wanted to come. And I know that his mom and dad are still in the colony. That they haven't yet joined the tent city. But the Sollomon's are rule-followers. They believe the Leadership Council would do no wrong, yet I've learned that even seemingly good people are capable of wrong-doing.

I want to say something reassuring and remind him that my finding the stone helps everyone in the long run. If I don't find it and defeat the Imminent Darkness, it isn't just one or two lives that will be lost, it will be an entire planet—possibly the entire Universe. That's a lot to swallow before breakfast.

"Time isn't the same here as it is there. We could be here a week and only a day will have passed back home." I leave out the part about him wanting to come with me in the first place.

There's a moment of silence and then Sloan says gently, "So a plan?"

"My vote is that when we arrive we immediately find the Chief Tonitrui. He's the one who will have the answers, but I don't think they'll be given easily."

"I second that vote," says Doran. "If only because I have no other plan."

"I don't suppose anyone would be interested in bypassing the Tonitrui and going in search of the stone on our own?" Li asks. "I'm not too interested in getting involved in someone else's political affairs."

"There's no choice really. The stone could be anywhere, and I've almost always relied on guidance of some kind in order to find it. Even if the Tonitrui are deceptive and even if there is something going on between them and the Fulgurs—and I'm not saying that there is because we don't know that yet—then maybe it would help us to find out more about Isa and exactly whose side she's on."

Cerise gives Li a sympathetic look. "Sorry, Sweets, but I'm going to have to agree with Kata and the others on this one. The Chief is going to have answers, and even if we don't like them, it will be better than going in with our eyes closed. I just hope—"

Her words are cut off as the ship lurches forward. The instrumental music cuts out and a loud warning signal begins to sound and the cockpit is flooded in a light of flashing white and red. Sloan grips the half-wall behind the benches as he makes his way to the control panel.

All the different buttons are lit up and flashing which I assume can't be good. He begins pressing buttons and moving levers. I drop my messenger bag over my head and hurry beside him. There's a panel lit up solid red with the words: DANGER in big, black capital letters.

"What's going on?" I ask, scanning the NS, but its screen has gone blank.

"I don't know." He pulls up a monitor and begins pressing buttons. A blueprint of the small ship pops up. In one of the back rooms down the hallway to the left is a big yellow X that's flashing. Sloan grabs the image and uses his fingers to zoom in on it.

The ship shakes and something from one of the storage rooms falls over with a *crash!*

"Uh, anytime, Captain!" Doran calls, his voice ringing with panic.

"I'm trying!" Sloan shouts over the racket of falling provision boxes. "That's the fuel room." He explains to me. "There's been a leak or something."

A voice comes over the warning signal. "Auto-pilot disengaged. Ship evacuation commence."

"Evacuation?" Li calls and the ship lurches forward again as Sloan grasps helplessly at the steering controls.

"There's a leak in the fuel room!" Sloan shouts above the noise. "We have to evacuate." He pulls the ship upward a bit. I peer out the windshield. We're still a ways above the sea. If we crash into the sea, how will we reach the Isle of Tonitrui? Could we swim? Or would we just drown—dying so far from home?

I didn't come this far to die here. Not now.

"There has to be a way to evacuate the ship." I move the monitor so that I can better see it and start searching through the digital files until I find a document entitled *Evacuation Procedures*.

"I'd say time is of the essence!" Li calls out helpfully.

"We have to get to the back of the ship. Near the ramp is a small, emergency escape pod." My eyes continue to rapidly scan the file, the words becoming a yellow blur on the black screen. "It's only meant to hold three people at a time, but it will have to do."

I turn and look at Li. "Go! You three go and get to the escape pod, Sloan will have to steer the ship until the pod's ready to go. As soon as he lowers the ramp we'll have to make a run for it."

Li scowls at me as he braces himself against the half-wall of the recessed area and the interior wall of the ship. "That sounds like a crap plan."

He sticks his hand in his pocket and pulls out a small, flesh-colored silicone disc. An ear piece. He hands it to me and I stick it into my ear as he does the same with a second identical piece. With a last, meaningful glance, he grabs Cerise's hand and they run after Doran who's already started down the center hallway.

"Can you give them enough time?" I ask Sloan, bracing myself on the dashboard with one hand and placing the other on his arm.

"I can try," he says, not taking his eyes off the sea in front of us.

Sloan uses the levers to nose the ship skyward. I can hear the soft pounding of feet in my ear piece and noises that sound like clanging metal. The whine of the alarm fills my ears. I'm pretty sure we'll both be partially deaf by the time we get out of here.

I move my hand back to the monitor and scan the information that's being sent from the sensors in the fuel room. Lethal levels of mentahilene. It's not a fuel I've ever heard of, but I suppose that doesn't matter if it can kill us. My fingers zoom in to a black container with a red X flashing over it. A leak. Little images of fire flames have begun popping up around the fuel room.

"Do you think this was an accident?" I ask Sloan, zooming out of the fuel room and going back to the blueprint of the ship. My eyes scanning for the escape pod.

"What else would it be?" Sloan asks, green eyes darting to me for a moment. The ship shakes and the monitor lets me know that one of the two engines has officially died. "We don't have much time."

"Li, where the hell are you guys? We've lost an engine."

"We've found the escape pod, and you weren't kidding about the three people. It's going to be quite cozy in here with the five of us," Li's voice is muffled.

"They're good," I tell Sloan. He pulls one of the levers all the way down, dropping the ship's ramp. The ship immediately nosedives at the distortion of balance.

"Go! I'm right behind you!" Sloan shouts. But I shake my head. Those are words I've heard before. Dangerous words.

I glance at the flashing lights and knobs on the control panel. My eyes glean the blank screen of the NS. I grab it, ripping it away from the control panel. I pull until the tangle of wires comes away with it and I'm left holding the thin, black box in my hand, wires dangling.

"Here we come!" Sloan hollers loud enough for Li to hear through the ear piece. He grabs my hand and we run, forced to slide this way and that as the ship tries to course correct itself. But it's no use with one engine and the fuel room on fire. Smoke is billowing out of the hallway on the far right. Sloan pulls his shirt up over his nose and mouth, and his eyes urge me to do the same. I slip the NS into my messenger bag, and use my free hand to pull my t-shirt up over my mouth and nose. We run down the center hallway, past the small kitchen area and the provision storage until we come to a skidding stop at a small docking area beside the ramp.

The dock holds a small, round bubble. Its hatch is still open. Sloan pulls me toward it, then lifts me up, practically dumping me through the hatch. I land awkwardly on top of Li, with my boot in his face. I barely have time to scramble out of the way before Sloan is dropping himself through the opening and pulling it closed behind him.

Doran is already positioned at the small control panel, he presses a lever and the small ship rolls forward and then to the left, placing itself on the ramp. We roll down slowly, the mother ship screaming behind us. The ship jostles roughly, probably as the other engine dies, and we glide down the ramp. Then we are airborne for only a moment before we're dropped roughly into the sea. My knee rams into Li's ribcage and my elbow into Cerise's cheek.

"Sorry," I mumble as I try to right myself.

Sloan climbs over the others to reach Doran. "What's going on?"

Doran shrugs. "I don't know. It has directions written over here, but it's all gibberish to me." He moves aside and Sloan slides into the captain's chair. He pushes some levers and moves some stuff around. The small bubble ship glides across the sea. From the outside, the ship appears to be solid black, but from the inside it's transparent and we can see out. I watch over Li's shoulder as the ship behind us grows smaller, until suddenly there's a thunderous boom, and orange-red flames shoot into the bloodied-charcoal sky.

Cerise is kneeling beside me, hazel eyes round with shock. "We only just…"

"I know," I whisper.

Then I feel a rush of panic as I see the large wave rushing toward us. I guess the impact had to go somewhere. "Sloan!"

He glances behind him and mumbles something that sounds like *oh, shit* before turning back around and fumbling with the controls. Cerise and I watch as the gray wave comes barreling toward us. Just as it's about to overcome our ship, we lurch upward and the wave continues on beneath us, unbroken.

"Oh my moons!" Cerise says, turning around and sinking into the seat cushion. "That was a close one."

"I think I have the hang of it now," Sloan says, not taking his eyes off the sky in front of him. "We're only working with a single engine now and a lot less weight due to the fact that there's no storage or provisions. That said we're also on a limited fuel supply."

The ship is small. The control panel is about half the size of the other ship and there's a captain's chair and two other chairs behind it. There's a narrow partition with a curtain and I assume that's the toilet. To the right of the toilet is a set of shelves enclosed in a glass box. It looks like a mix of first aid and emergency provisions. But that's it. There's nothing else to the ship. The sea stretches for kilometers below us and the sky for kilometers above us.

I climb over the two chairs and pull the NS out of my messenger bag. With Doran's help we hook it up to one of the small power hubs on the control panel. At first only a blank screen stares back at us, but then it flashes a couple of times as it boots up. Then, like magic, the screen appears and spits out some coordinates. We've only slightly deviated from our original course. Still we have another 1.3 tetras to go.

And that's if nothing else goes wrong.

CHAPTER 15

Sloan has set the ship to autopilot, but unlike the last one, no instrumental music begins to play. Instead it's just silence. All around us is inky blackness. The silvery stars are out and tonight the indigo moon is full casting everything in a soft, purple glow. It's disorienting to look out and see everything from every direction, but at the same time it also makes me feel safer.

Cerise and Li are asleep, curled up together in one of the chairs. Her head is resting on his shoulder and I can hear Li's soft snoring. Doran is asleep in the other chair, arms and legs all sprawled out. Sloan stands, between the dashboard and the captain's chair, hands clasped behind him, just staring out at the darkness.

I squeeze myself beside him, wrapping my arms around his waist and resting my chin on his shoulder. I'm pretty tall and Sloan is only a few inches taller than me. His familiar smell of leather, soap, and sea greets me. Even without the Water coursing through his body, the salty scent of it still lingers on his skin and in his hair. His hair is so long now it's begun to curl at the nape of his neck. He leans back into me, but still doesn't take his gaze from the emptiness before us.

"You were amazing back there," I whisper, careful not to wake the others. But after the day's adventure I'm not sure that they'll be all that easy to wake up anyways.

"Thanks. It was still a close call though. If Doran hadn't thought fast and began to steer us…or if we had only been a few minutes slower, who knows what…" He shakes his head at what might have happened.

"You never answered me earlier." I prod gently. "About it being an accident."

"If it's not an accident, then that would mean it was intentional. Do you think your Aunt Isa is so similar to your Aunt Tullia?" He looks down at me and his eyes cloud over at his mention of the Water Queen.

"I'm not sure. Maybe not Isa…but remember when we left? Aama said something strange. He said that he hoped our journey was unhindered with difficulties."

He shrugs beneath my chin. "The Fulgurs seem to have a peculiar way with words."

I decide not to push the issue any further. I know that Sloan thinks I too easily jump to conclusions, without examining all the evidence first. Like I did with the Leadership Council. And even though no one's stepped out and said, *"Hi there, we're working for the Imminent Darkness, just so you know!"* All the pieces of the puzzle are beginning to slide together: the prisoners kept beneath Council Hall, the creepy statue of the codger in its courtyard, the strange *divide et impera* archway at the University Complex, Finn's arrest and wrongful imprisonment, and not to mention the fact that they've done nothing to stop the so-called Citizen Law Enforcement, the same people who are clearly being influenced by the ID and it's poisonous dark energy. But am I right about this too? Does someone in the Land of Metal not want me to succeed? Or am I being used as a pawn in a game too complex for my own understanding.

I let out an involuntary sigh of frustration.

"You should rest." Sloan misinterprets my sigh as tiredness. I suppose I am tired. Tired of being lied to and misled, tired of people using me for their own personal gain. Sloan sits in the captain's chair and pulls me into his lap. I yawn and lay my head down onto his shoulder. He strokes my hair as he continues to stare out at the vast night. I close my eyes and for once try not to think about ulterior motives and alternate agendas. I slip into a dreamless sleep.

. . .

When I wake up, I'm still curled in the captain's chair, but Sloan is standing at the controls staring off into the blood-red abyss. I feel a pang of sadness. I miss home. Home the way it used to be. Going to school—okay, no, I don't miss that part. I miss things being normal. I miss my mom and dad being under the same roof as me. I miss my mom being overprotective and my dad coming home late from work as a liege to the Council. I miss swinging on the swings with Ahna and Li pestering me to go to the Black Bazaar with him. I miss sharing secrets and stolen kisses. I miss being ordinary.

Sloan's draped a zipper hoodie around me like a blanket. His angular face is cast in a red shadow and the side that used to have his scales—the mark of a Water Elemental—is smooth as baby skin, as if nothing had ever been there. The light catches the faint scar down his neck. A faded reminder. His shoulders are back and his fingers gracefully move over the controls, not doing anything as the autopilot is engaged, but as if he's going through the motions of landing the ship when we arrive at the Isle of the Tonitrui later tonight.

No, I don't miss everything. Because if things were the way they used to be—if I was simply an ordinary girl studying her chosen Elemental—I never would have gotten to know Sloan in this intimate way. I'd never have felt my heart swell at his touch, at the sound of his voice. I'd never have felt the terrifying feeling of possibly losing him forever. And I wouldn't have become friends with Cerise or Doran. I wouldn't have met so many people who are unbelievably kind and selfless. I would never have realized how good people can be. No. I don't miss everything.

Sloan turns and catches me watching him. He smiles sheepishly. "Just going over the landing."

"It should be easy for you. Everything else about flying seems to be." I stand up and hand his hoodie back to him, but he shakes his head so I drape it over the back of the Captain's chair.

"If there had been a Wind Elemental maybe that's what I would have chosen. I've never felt called to something as much as I feel called to the air." He drapes an arm around my shoulder.

I think of the Zephyrus Seeds and the numerous times that I was able to summon the wind and ask for its safe transport in and around the Elemental Abyss. "Maybe someday there could be." I intertwine my fingers with his.

"New Elementals? Now that would certainly throw the Imminent Darkness into a tizzy," Doran says as he scours the shelf near the first aid kit before plucking something up that looks like crackers. "This is just sad."

"The escape pod wasn't meant for a long journey. It had to be compact to fit within the mother ship. We're lucky it was there."

"Or *ka-boom*!" Li says throwing his hands up into the air. Cerise stands behind him, squeezed between the chair and transparent wall of the ship. She pats him on the shoulders.

"That's right. The big ship went bye-bye," she says in a voice like she were talking to a small child.

"All kidding aside," Doran says as he bites into a stack of crackers, crumbs tumbling to the floor. "Do we stick to the plan for when we arrive? From what you've told me, and the more I think about it, the Tonitrui don't sound like they're exactly going to have out the welcoming committee."

"He has a point. We don't even know if they know that we're coming," Li says.

"And Isa didn't exactly seem like the type who would tell them," Cerise adds.

All these unknown variables make me nervous. I'd thought of the Tonitrui not being welcoming, possibly even being hostile, but I hadn't thought much past that. What had Bina said? That I should gain their respect and trust, but not the other way around. That if I could learn their secrets, I could have their power. Which begs the question, what secrets does Isa want to find out and what ones does she want to protect?

"I say we go in just with that thought. We can't assume they're expecting us, it could be dangerous to assume that. So I think we should go in cautiously and gracefully," Sloan says. Doran sidesteps back and forth, sweeping his arms like a dancer this way and that.

He says in a very proper voice, "Cautiously and gracefully. Cautiously and gracefully." He looks ridiculous.

"You can go in that way," I say to him. "We'll send you in first and see how it works out."

Doran scowls and throws the empty cracker box at me. "You're never any fun."

"Sticks and stones," I reply, but I can't help but smile.

. . .

The indigo moon is high above the horizon and the sky is back to its stormy, charcoal gray. Lightning flashes followed by thunderous booms so loud, it feels as though our tiny bubble ship tremors with each one. If the Fulgurs are lightning people, then I wonder what thunder people look like. I suppose I'm about to find out.

A gray edge has appeared at the horizon. Land. I pace back and forth in the narrow space behind Sloan, fingering the bullet that still hangs around my neck. The bullet that was meant to kill me, but didn't. Instead it was given new life and brought us here. Maybe it's good luck. If you believe in that sort of thing. Part of me thinks that believing in luck is the kind of thinking that gets you killed.

The ship has begun a slow descent, so that we approach land coming in at an angle. It's windier on this side of the sea. Below us the waves are white-capped swells. The little ship shakes against the wind. I can't imagine how we're going to travel the 2.3 tetras back to Isa's in this bubble. I chew on my thumbnail as we lower altitude, Sloan's hands steadily manipulating the controls.

I glance at the NS. The land we're approaching is shaped like a crescent, we're entering into a bay like area. From the topography, it doesn't appear that there are mountains here, just flat land which should make for easy landing for Sloan. Thunder booms and shakes the ship as we drop again. I grip the dashboard for stability.

My heart begins to pound with the combination of adrenaline and anxiety. I silently whisper a hope to the Universe that we aren't walking right into some kind of trap, and that the Tonitrui can truly help me find the Metal stone. Bonus points, I think, if they can help me to destroy it.

The shaking of the ship increases as we continue our descent. Li and Cerise are each buckled into the two passenger chairs, which came equipped with harnesses. Doran is in some kind of harness contraption that's located on the wall near the back of the ship. There are three. The other two hang empty.

In order to land the ship, Sloan has to stay at the control panel, so I buckle myself into the captain's chair. Which really isn't all that practical since the captain spends most of his time standing, except for when the ship is on autopilot. Maybe the Fulgurs have more faith in their ships piloting capabilities than we do.

There's no automated voice to tell us that we're approaching our destination, but with the transparent walls of the ship we can all see the dark mass of land rising out of the sea before us. Tall, jagged structures stick out of the landscape. They glisten in the moonlight. The waves crash onto the shore, which is blanketed with brilliant, blood-red sand. We approach rapidly. Sloan instructs us to hold on and he begins the last of his descent, skidding the bottom of the bubble across the sea for a couple of beats, before we're briefly airborne once again, and then sliding across the red sand until we come to a stop.

Every one lets out a collective breath, one that we'd apparently all been holding. Sloan has a bead of sweat at his temple, but he's smiling. I unbuckle my harness and throw my arms around his neck, planting a kiss on his lips.

"You did it! We landed and we're all in one piece!" I grin and he lifts me up in a hug, my feet dangling in the air.

"Yeah, but where the heck are we?" Doran asks, unfastening himself and peering out the walls at the strange beach. Sloan sets me down gently and we follow Doran's gaze.

The tall, glistening structures resemble black prisms. All angular sides and tilted this way and that, as if someone haphazardly stuck them in the ground.

"Those almost look like gemstones," Li says unbuckling himself.

"Or crystals. They're beautiful," Cerise says. Then she pauses and points. "But what's that there?"

Out of the crystal forest the silhouette of a bulky creature appears on the beach. Followed by another and another. And another. Doran was wrong.

They did send out the welcoming committee after all.

CHAPTER 16

My boots sink into the sand as we walk toward the row of gargantuan creatures. What is it with this place and ridiculously tall beings? They appear androgynous, much like the Fulgurs. Except instead of tall and thin-limbed, these beings are tall as well as wide. One Tonitrui is easily two or three Fulgurs wide.

Their skin is as gray as the mountains from whence we came. Their heads are jagged and bald. Their muscles bulge against their skin, as if trying to claw through it. They hold spears with a dark gray tip and large, silver disc-shaped shields. Their lips are large and wide, pulled across flat, rock-like teeth. They have wide, flat noses and hooded eyes. Behind the hoods, the eyes are a gray that is a shade lighter than their skin tone. If people were chiseled out of stone instead of flesh, this is what I imagine the end result would be.

I take a deep breath, glancing at Sloan for reassurance. He gives me an imperceptible nod, so I step forward. I take another deep breath in the hopes that my voice won't come out in a childish squeak, because let's be honest, I'd rather be climbing back into the ship right about now and flying off into the night sky.

I clear my throat. "I am Ka. Niece of Isa, Goddess of Metal, Queen of this Land. I have come to seek your help with the Metal stone." I tilt my chin slightly, so that my head is bowed. I know that I need to appear strong, respectful, and trustworthy. The less I say, the more likely I am to pull that off.

There's a deep rumble of laughter as one of the Tonitrui steps forward. I assume he is the Chief. He somehow appears even larger than the others and on his head he wears a metal helmet that comes down over his hooded eyes but stops above his nose, resting across his cheekbones. I wonder how he doesn't sink into the sand from his sheer size alone.

"Isa is no queen of ours," he says and his voice is deep and booming. It reverberates in my ears long after he stops speaking. First the constant buzzing, now this. What is it with this place? I raise my head at his words, remembering both Isa and Bina's advice about the Tonitrui's cunning way with words.

"Maybe not. But she is the Metal Goddess, therefore she has dominion over this planet, if I'm not mistaken. And very rarely am I mistaken." I'm not sure where the burst of confidence comes from, because I fear if I glance down at my knees they'd be knocking together from fright. Maybe it's the compulsion to defend my family, whether I like them or not. Either way, I hope that I haven't stepped too far out of line. Leave it to me to shoot myself in the foot before I've even had a chance to look around.

The Chief snarls. "You are arrogant, just as she is. But you are correct. She may fancy herself the queen of the Fulgurs, but she will never be the queen of the Tonitrui."

The Chief stabs the blunt end of his spear into the ground and the other Tonitrui roar in approval. It's a frightening sound resembling the rumble of thunder. Lightning flashes overhead, momentarily cloaking the beach in white light. The faces of the Tonitrui momentarily captured in twisted sneers.

"The Tonitrui are an independent people. That is why we inhabit this land across the sea. Come, girl who calls herself Ka. Let us discuss this stone that you seek and how you may best serve us."

The Chief turns and the rest of the tribe pause, waiting for me to follow. I don't look behind me, don't want them to see me seeking approval from the others in case they view it as a weakness. Earn their respect and their trust. Learn their secrets. Secrets are power.

I hold my head high, making eye contact with as many of the Tonitrui as I can as I fall into step behind the Chief. Sloan and the others are behind me and I can sense the rest of the Tonitrui falling into step around us.

The beach transitions into jagged rows of the dark gray gemstone with cleared walkways every few feet, almost like narrow roads. My boots make no sound over the flat, black ground as I follow the Chief toward a long building with a flat roof, except for a single rounded dome in its center. It has a stone overhang, and the building itself is supported by thick, stone columns. The crystal gems stop at a ring of black ground that surrounds the building. The dirt sparkles in the moonlight, as if maybe it is the same crystals ground up into teeny, tiny, microscopic pieces.

There are no windows or doors. The building is just open air. We walk through a long hallway of polished white stone until we reach a large room with the domed ceiling. The room is circular and embedded in the center of the floor is a shiny, metal five-pointed star. At the topmost point of the star rests a massive chair entirely made out of stone, all in one piece with no joints or hinges. The Chief lumbers toward it. He removes his helmet and hands it to another Tonitrui standing nearby, along with his shield. He keeps the spear. He sits on the throne and the five of us stand awkwardly in the center of the room, on top of the metallic star. The Chief has a commanding presence, much more intimidating than Isa draped so casually across her throne. I wait for him to address me.

"So, it is the Metal stone that you seek. And, pray tell, how do you think that I, of all creatures, could possibly help you with such a task?" The Chief's voice rumbles through the empty chamber.

"I was told that you would know. That you are cunning and wise," I reply. Sloan flanks my one side and Li the other, with Doran and Cerise standing beside them and somewhat behind. I have no weapons. No defense of any kind, except my Elemental powers. One weapon I do have is my words, and I don't know a single person who doesn't like to be flattered.

The Chief smiles, at least I think it's a smile. It's somewhere between a grimace and a grin. "That is true. But you see, your queen and I are not allies."

"She's not my queen. She's my aunt," I correct. "There's a difference."

The Chief nods, leaning on the hilt of his spear. His pale eyes are discerning. "That is true. One is fealty by choice and the other is fealty by blood." He pauses and I realize that he's waiting for a response. The word *trickster* keeps looping through my mind. Truth be told I'm not the talker of the group. I'm not witty nor quick with words.

There was this girl Diadona, who made my life a living hell in school. She was always saying nasty things to me and knocking my books off my desk, all while batting her eyelashes at Sloan when he was our Universal History teacher. I never had the nerve to say anything to her. I'd always think of the best retorts hours later when I was hanging out with Ahna, because around Ahna I could say what I wanted and she wouldn't laugh at me. So I take my time formulating a response that will be just as precise in language as the Chief's.

"At least you know then that I didn't make a bad choice." I raise an eyebrow at him and this time he lets out a long, boisterous laugh that rattles the building. I feel Sloan beside me let out a breath he must have been holding.

"You are not foolish, I'll give you that. Now, tell me about your purpose for seeking this stone as well as my help."

"The Imminent Darkness has taken over my home, the planet of

Xon 9. The stones were gifted to me upon my birth and then later used to protect me. Now in order to prevent the Imminent Darkness from creating Universal chaos, I need to destroy each stone and restore my birthright back to me. The Metal stone is the last one that I need to find."

The Chief nods as if he knew all of this already and was merely playing along as if it's his expected role. "The Imminent Darkness threatens all of us, with its uncertainty and anarchy. My people like structure."

That explains a lot as to why they don't get along with Isa. Isa is the antithesis of structure and order. It's more like all night raves and hung over mornings.

"The stone itself is easy enough to find. But what can I expect in return from you for helping you to find it?" He pauses as if deep in thought. "Fealty? Blood?"

Actually, I'm hoping for neither of those things, I think. *Maybe I was just going to try my luck that deep down, past that stony exterior, you're just a really nice guy.*

"I am not a resident of this land, as you know, and so it would be dishonest to swear fealty to someone someplace other than my home. But I will offer you blood in exchange for help finding the Metal stone." I hear Cerise let out a little gasp behind me.

"So be it then. Blood will be your price. I will help you to find the Metal stone." The Chief raps his spear against the floor as if it confirms our agreement.

. . .

The Chief wastes no time. He assigns one of his tribe to be our guide. He's a creature of few words named Magna. The indigo moon is high in the sky and I'm thankful that we slept at least a little bit last night because it doesn't look like sleep is on the agenda.

Magna leads us into what I've come to think of as the crystal forest. Dark gray gemstones grow like trees from the black ground, like fingers of the dead clawing for the sun. I let out a shiver. Sloan puts an arm around my shoulders and gives me a squeeze. Magna stops and turns. Because he is so large and thick, it's like watching time move backwards.

"Hematite."

His voice is a low tenor that rumbles at the end. Then he turns back around, his boulder-like feet sinking into the ground with each step, to only have the black soil bounce back, leaving no visible trace. Splashes of lightning illuminate the sky followed by the boom of thunder.

"Is he talking about the crystals?" I ask, lowering my voice.

"I think so. Bina used crystals sometimes, but I didn't always pay attention."

Sloan reaches out a hand to touch one of the plant-like sculptures. Grimacing, he immediately yanks his hand away, a thin slice of blood drips down his index finger. He jams his finger into his mouth, stanching the flow of blood.

Crystals sharp as knives. People who look as though they're made of stone. The one thing Isa and the Tonitrui seem to have in common is a penchant for dangerous landscapes. We continue walking for maybe a half hour more when Magna suddenly draws up short.

He's stopped in front of a small cavern that's surrounded by hematite trees, obscuring its entrance from view.

"The Metal stone you speak of is in here." He points into the darkness. Of course it is.

He steps into the darkness feeling along the wall and comes back with a lantern. Then he reaches into a pouch on his belt that sheathes his dagger. His fingers glisten with something like liquid silver. He opens the lantern's little door and slides the silver into it. The lantern glows with starlight. Magna hands it to me.

I take it. "You're not coming?"

He gives a slow shake of his head. "Magna stay here and wait."

Li steps forward and peers into the cave. "You must be scared."

Magna laughs and it's like a roll of thunder. "No. Not scared. Also, not stupid." He crosses his massive arms to indicate it's the end of the discussion.

"Great," I mumble. "Just when things were beginning to go so well." I hold the lantern up to illuminate the darkness and step into the cavern.

CHAPTER 17

The site that greets us takes my breath away. The cavern's sides and ceiling are made of hematite, beautiful glistening gray-black stone that matches the night sky. Li, Sloan, Cerise, and Doran fold in around me. I hold the lantern high, but the starlight doesn't cast a very large pool of light. We take a few tentative steps.

"Try not to touch the walls. The edges can be sharp," I remind everyone.

The cavern slopes downward, but it's gradual. My boots sink into the spongey earth and somewhere I can hear the distant drip of water.

"Do you think this could be a trap?" Doran asks, a trace of trepidation in his voice.

I shrug, the lantern bouncing off the prisms all around us. "I suppose it could be. But what would they get out of it? The Tonitrui don't want the Imminent Darkness endangering the Universe as much as we don't want it ruining Xon 9. As far as I know, I'm the only shot they've got."

We're all pressed together, trying to let the lantern's meek light guide us. The darkness is so black that it feels like the nothingness is pushing in from all sides. We round a corner and a shrill cry stops my blood cold. It sounds inhuman.

This wouldn't be the first land in which I've met monsters.

"What was that?" Cerise whispers, clutching my shoulder.

Sloan has a dagger sheathed beneath his pant leg and I wouldn't doubt that each of the others has a weapon somewhere on their person. The Tonitrui never searched us when we emerged from our ship. I am most likely the only weaponless one, relying solely on my Elemental powers of Earth, Fire, Wood, and Water. Although in a situation like this only the Earth and the Fire would be of any help. What would I do? Truth the monster to death? Terrorize it with its future?

There's another shrill shriek followed by a rush of wind coming at us from the back of the cavern. The rush of wind is rank with a foul stench, like someone who hasn't showered in months: dirt and filth, maybe a little bit of rot and mold thrown in for good measure.

"That smells like death," Li says coughing into his shirt.

"I was thinking it smelled more like you after a training session," Cerise replies.

"Ha. Ha. Ha," Li grumbles. "Everyone's so full of wit and charm

200

today."

His last words are overtaken by a new sound, the sound of canvas flapping in the wind. No, not canvas. My brain rapidly tries to sort through images, experiences I've had in distant lands. Birds. But this doesn't sound like any bird I've ever heard before. The sound gets louder, followed by more shrieks. The shrieks crescendo until it sounds as though they're right above our heads and Sloan shoves me to the ground, covering my body with his own.

Wind rushes over us. Sloan isn't covering my head, just my body, and I can feel something warm and furry bounce off the back of my head. It sends another shiver down my spine. The lantern fell when Sloan shoved me, but it's still lit. I dare to glance up. I can see a snout and beady eyes in a squished-looking face. The monster has pointy ears, a large, furry body, and huge wings that seem to easily reach from one side of the cavern to the other. It's as large as or larger than a Tonitrui. Again, what is it with this land and giant things?

"A bat." Sloan's breath is warm in my ear. On Xon 9 we don't really have animals. It's difficult enough to support the human population, let alone other species. Unless of course, they're grown in a controlled environment like our food sources. But I vaguely recall learning about bats in Earth Biology.

"Nocturnal," I whisper back. The shrieking fades away as the bat soars to the front of the cavern. No wonder Magna said he wasn't scared, just not stupid. Only a fool would venture into a cave with bats large enough to eat them for breakfast, lunch, or dinner.

The cavern falls into silence once again and Sloan rolls off me, then helps me to my feet. He picks up the lantern.

"What the hell was that?" Doran asks. Apparently, he did not pay attention in Earth Biology.

"That was a bat," Sloan answers. "It's a nocturnal animal. Usually, they're not meat-eaters."

"Well, that's a relief," Cerise says getting up and dusting her shirt off.

"They're also not usually as big as a trailer either."

"Nocturnal. So, they see best at night. Hunt at night. How convenient that we were sent here at night," Li says.

"Do you think there are more?" I ask.

Sloan shrugs. "They could just reside in here. Bats on Old Earth lived in caves. But, they could also be here to protect the stone." He takes my hand and pulls me along down the path, deeper into the cavern.

"I'm going with the latter," Doran says following behind me.

The path narrows and the light from the lantern falls onto an open space just ahead of us. In the center of the space is a cluster of jagged hematite stones. The stones form a circle around a perfectly round, smooth-looking gray stone perched on a column of white stone. My body seems to buzz in response to its presence, knowing before my brain can even comprehend that we've found the Metal stone.

"Doesn't it seem strange that it seems so…unprotected?" Doran asks, most likely remembering our venture into the center of an active volcano in order to retrieve the Fire stone. But looks can be

202

deceiving. As soon as the Fire stone was lifted from its pedestal, the volcano erupted shooting fire, ash, and rock into the sky.

The Metal stone shines in the silver starlight, like a glowing beacon beckoning me to it. Destroying this stone—the last of the five—is the missing piece to the puzzle that is Ka. It will restore my personality from its fractured parts into something whole again. Li would argue that I was never not whole to begin with. But he doesn't understand. I, myself, didn't even understand until my Elements started being returned to me. It's like finding a long-lost relative. You weren't sad because you didn't know they were missing, but as soon as they return to your life you wonder how you ever lived without them in it. And I'm actually not sure how I made it this long being only a wisp of my true self.

I take a step forward, drawn to the stone by some force beyond my simple human understanding. But Sloan puts out an arm to stop me.

"It isn't unprotected," he whispers, his voice soft and even, answering Doran's question. I give him a confused look. It's sitting right there out in the open. Ripe for the taking. But Sloan's remembered what I've forgotten in my haste for the stone— that the Tonitrui are cunning.

He raises the lantern and the light falls on a beam of hematite stretched across the ceiling of the cavern, above the Metal stone's pedestal. Hanging upside down from the beam are several large, furry bats as big as houses. And our presence has just woken them up.

. . .

The sound is deafening as I drop to the floor, pulling Cerise down with me. We scramble to the side of the cavern, seeking refuge near the wall. Furry bodies hover over us. Giant, leathery wings beat the top of my head, tangling in my hair and pulling at my ponytail. Sloan tries to wave the lantern at the beasts, but the starlight is too dim.

"Wait!" I call out. My voice is immediately drowned out by the echoing cry of the bats. I flip open my messenger bag and pull out a flashlight. I'd forgotten that I had it all along. I was never really all that great at school, but I remember some of the basic, common-sense sorts of things. Like nocturnal animals hunt at night because they don't like the light.

A massive bat is hovered above Sloan, its claws entangled in his chestnut-colored hair. He's helplessly waving around the lantern. Ever the bold one, or stupid depending on how you look at it, Li runs toward the creature waving his arms and screaming like a maniac. But it has no affect. Several of the bats had flown down the path and out toward the cave's opening, but two bats remain. The one hovering over the stone, using its giant wings to try and pull Sloan away from it. And a second bat that has Doran pinned against the wall as he hits at it with his fists, then an elbow. But it seems to have no effect. No amount of training has prepared us for this.

I flip on the flashlight and aim its beam at the bat above Sloan. The light illuminates its squished face and pointy ears. The beam finds its beady eyes and it lets out a strangled cry of protest. Disentangling its claws from Sloan's hair and trying to back away. It lets out an angry gurgle. I keep the flashlight aimed at its eyes, trying to blind it at least long enough for us to grab the stone and run like heck out of here. The bat flaps angrily against the wall, screeching, trying to use its echolocation to search out its prey.

Sloan recovers quickly. He dives for the pedestal, gracefully snatching up the stone and clenching it into his fist as though it's the most prized of possessions. There's a loud screech behind me and I whirl around to shine the flashlight on the bat near Doran. Cerise let's out a crazed war cry and before I can figure out what's happening she's stabbing at the giant beast with a dagger that must have been hidden in the tangles of her red hair. The bat lets out a screech and backs away. Dark blood drips to the black floor. It doesn't look enough to kill it, just to wound it and give us enough time to run for our lives.

Cerise grabs Doran's hand and doesn't wait for him to get to his feet before she's bolting down the passageway, the dagger still clenched in her free hand. Sloan and I sprint after her with Li bringing up the rear. The lantern is left behind, dropped to the floor in the bat scuffle. The flashlight beam bounces off the hematite walls. I can hear the distant, angry screeches of the bats behind us and the deep roll of thunder somewhere in front of us.

The darkness shifts and I can see the cavern opening only a little ways before us. I feel the rush of wind behind us and know that the bats have found the way out. The screeching grows louder and the evening light grows brighter. It's strange to be able to feel something coming before you can see it. It's as though I can feel the weight of the beast manipulating the space above me. Claws entangle in my hair. I let out a yelp. Doran, Cerise, and Sloan have already made it out of the cave.

I try to make a dive for the opening, but a bat snatches me away with its giant claws. I feel my feet being lifted off the ground, and then I feel something else pulling me in the opposite direction back toward the ground. A heavy weight and tight, sure fingers are wrapped around my boot. I look down and see a mess of black hair. Li. The bat's claws sink into either of my shoulders and I can feel the blood soaking through my shirt. I'm being stretched in two different directions. The bat tries to pull me up and out of the cave opening, but Li is pulling as hard as he can in the opposite direction, skidding across the ground, trying to find his footing.

The musty stench makes me want to gag. Dumbly, I try to aim the flashlight at the bat's face but it's too far away. I twist and jerk, trying to get it to loosen its grip and drop me, but it only digs its claws in deeper. Li is losing his grip.

"Help her!" Cerise yells at Magna.

But even from above I can see Magna's shrug and hear his deep voice respond, "Magna only told to help find stone. Magna not told to save girl's life."

"That girl is going to save all your lives, but she won't be able to if she's dead!" Cerise argues hotly. She shoves the dagger in his direction. I have to admire her fiery spirit.

Fire.

"Let go!" I yell down to Li. He looks at me as if I'm crazy, and maybe I am because there's the possibility that what I'm about to do will break every bone in my body. But I'm half-immortal right? It most likely won't kill me. It will just hurt very, very badly.

Li let's go just like I knew he would, because he's that type of friend. The bat senses the change in weight and begins to draw me higher. I need to act fast. I summon up my Fire, feeling the surge of anger and frustration that often accompanies it. The feeling courses through my veins, lighting me up from the inside out, as though someone's took a match to some gasoline. My body is raging, waiting for a fight. The energy around me crackles in response to the shift. I feel like I'm burning up from the inside out and in one gigantic surge, the Fire pulses through me like a thunder clap. There's a flash of brilliant white light. The bat loosens its grip. I hear the sound of fabric ripping and then I'm free-falling through the air to the ground below.

CHAPTER 18

I'm expecting to hit solid ground, but instead it's like I'm absorbed, enfolded into the ground and then spit back up. The strange, spongey earth has swallowed me and spit me back out. Sloan helps me to my feet, the Metal stone still clutched in his hand. His face is unreadable as he inspects my torn shirt and the puncture marks from the bat's claws. Then he enfolds me in a hug, pulling me tight against his chest. His mouth is pressed to my hair which is a tangled knot, but he says nothing. Just holds me for several beats against the rise and fall of his breath before letting me go. He pushes the Metal stone into my hand.

"I think this is yours."

Magna is already walking away, lumbering back the way we came. Doran hurries after him, taking giant steps. Cerise shakes her head, tying her dagger back up into her hair and begins to follow.

Li clips me on the back. "You had me going for a second there. But way to do your Fire trick." He gives me a lop-sided grin before jogging up to join Cerise. He lowers his voice, but I can still hear him say, "The way you handled that beast, Babe. Fierce." Then he makes a ridiculous growl. Cerise giggles and elbows him in the ribs.

"What was he talking about, Fire trick?" I ask Sloan. Sloan has a fairly good understanding of my Elemental powers and how they work.

He looks at me for a moment, green eyes revealing nothing. Then says, "I'm not sure." But when he says it, his face looks like it goes out of focus for just a fraction of a second before returning to normal. It's my Water gift telling me that what he just said isn't the truth. I stare at him for a second, confused. I think it's the first time Sloan's ever out right lied to me.

. . .

I try not to let the fact that Sloan lied bother me. But it's kind of hard when you trust someone with everything you have. He took an Everlasting Vow to protect me, I reason with myself as we walk silently following Magna through the hematite grove. Maybe this lie is a protection. Even so it doesn't make me happy.

My shoulders throb. I try to ignore it. Instead, I turn the graphite-colored stone over in my palm. It's cool to the touch with smooth edges and flat sides. It's beautiful and mysterious much like the Land that it came from. A sliver of the blood sun has appeared at the horizon and the indigo moon has begun to fade into the charcoal sky.

210

I slip the stone into my pants pocket.

Over the hematite trees I see the dome gleaming a pinkish-white in the morning sun. Thunder rumbles. My stomach tightens. Isa knew that I needed the Metal stone, but somehow I can't shake the feeling that there's more to it than that. There has to be a reason that Isa and the Fulgurs live on one side of the sea and the Tonitrui live almost 2.5 days' time away by flying ship. Bina had said to earn their respect in order to learn the secrets of the Tonitrui. Secrets are power. What secrets does the Metal Goddess want to learn? More importantly, why does she want to learn them?

I can't shake the feeling that there's more here at stake than just me restoring my fractured personality. Someone's not telling the truth, and not just Sloan. Isa is keeping secrets, but so are the Tonitrui. And I plan on finding out just what those secrets are. But first, I promised the Chief blood instead of fealty. So, blood he shall have. Only, it won't be mine.

. . .

After I'm cleaned up and my shoulder wounds are disinfected and bandaged, we're led back into the great domed room. The Chief sits in his white stone throne and this time we're not alone. Surrounding the outer perimeter, interspersed among the columns, are Tonitrui, forming a large walled circle with us in its center.

"You have found the Metal stone?" the Chief asks.

I bow slightly. "Yes. I have retrieved the Metal stone. I thank you for your assistance in locating it."

The Chief nods. "I am glad. And now for your end of the

bargain. Blood." He pounds the blunt end of his spear onto the stone floor and the other Tonitrui begin to chant, soft and deep at first then growing louder until it's a gregarious roar like thunder.

"As you wish," I reply.

Several of the Tonitrui step forward. The Chief rises from his throne and raises his spear above his head. He lets out a deafening roar. So loud that strands of my hair actually blows back from my face and I can smell the decay on his breath. The surrounding Tonitrui roar in response. Several loose stones tumble from the dome above us, crumbling apart as they hit the floor.

Sloan gives me a mischievous look and I shrug knowingly. The Chief brings his spear down with a thunderous thud and the Tonitrui begin stomping their gigantic stone-sized feet. As they do, more stones tumble down. The columns surrounding us begin to sway back and forth. There's a sound as if the sky is ripping itself apart, and boulders begin to fall from the domed ceiling. It is raining stone among the Tonitrui's chant of: "Blood! Blood! Blood!"

I turn to the others. "Run!" I yell, the sound of my voice lost in the avalanche that has begun around us.

Stones are falling, columns swaying. It's only moments before the first one is ripped loose and falls against the one beside it, knocking a Tonitrui flat onto his stomach. There's a howl of pain as the column lands on top of him, crushing him. Another Tonitrui is hit in the head by a boulder that knocks him sideways. A crack—a cut?—forms and black blood oozes out of it, down the side of his face as he falls to one knee.

Not my blood. Not today.

We throw our arms up over our heads, even though it offers little protection from the crumbling building, and run out past the swaying columns, narrowly missing one that falls over. Its top is lodged against the column beside it, creating a triangular space for us to dash through.

A small boulder tumbles from above and knocks into Cerise, sending her sprawling forward. She rolls out of the way just in time, to prevent it from pinning her to the ground. Without slowing down, I grab her hand and we run after the others, back toward the red sand beach. Breaths ragged, angry roars echo behind us like shadows. Hot pain sears through my hamstring, but I run as if my life depends on it. Basically, because it does.

The sun is now high in the sky, everything bathed in blood red. Crashing, rumbling and angry shouts of protest fill the still morning air. The hematite trees do not bend or sway, but stand sentry as witness to the destruction I unwittingly just caused.

"Now what?" asks Doran, bent over with his hands on his knees trying to catch his breath. Despite his training, he only recently recovered from some cracked ribs from one of our other adventures.

"We go home," I reply holding up the bullet necklace.

"What about Isa?" asks Li, his hands clasped over his head as he tries to catch his breath, pacing back and forth.

"What about her? She wasn't much help to us, except to tell us the Chief Tonitrui would know where to find the stone. And I can't be sure she isn't the one who rigged our ship to catch fire. She can't be trusted. Besides I'm not here to solve her problems. Even if she is family."

I level a look at Sloan and Cerise, because unlike the others they know exactly what I'm talking about. Sometimes you may be tied to people by blood, but blood isn't what makes someone family. These people standing here on this strange beach with me in another land, we share no blood. But they are still my family.

Sloan casts a dejected glance back at our little, beached, bubble ship. Then he grabs hold of my hand. "Right. Let's go home."

Doran steps forward and takes Sloan's hand, followed by Cerise and Li, who links his arm through mine, so my hand is still free. I grab hold of the small bullet hanging from my neck.

"One thing though," Li says. "How did you know that would happen? That the building would collapse?"

I shrug. "I didn't."

Then I close my eyes and think of all the people waiting for me back home, counting on me to succeed. Mrs. Chatfield. Zora. Bax. Finn and Bina. My heart swells. No, family is not only bound by blood and DNA. Family is bound by so much more than that. It's bound by trust and loyalty and shared experiences. But most of all it is bound by love. As we're ripped from the Land of Metal, its thunderous roars fading into oblivion, and thrown into the nothingness, I think of home. The secrets of this land kept hidden for another time.

CHAPTER 19

The landing spills us out onto ground hard as concrete. Not the soft sponginess of the Land of the Tonitrui. I groan as I roll over onto my left side, cradling my messenger bag against me. More soft groans come from around me as the others check for broken bones or sprains. Most likely, the worst of it is some bruising and having the wind knocked out of you.

"Man, I just got these ribs fixed!" groans Doran.

"Don't be such a weakling," Li replies and I hear the rustle of leaves as Li helps him to his feet. I push myself to seated and look around, biting my tongue from telling him that we can't all be immortal like he is. The right time will come. He has to know. I will tell him. But not right now.

The necklace didn't take us to the tent city as I assumed it would, but it's gotten us close enough. We've been unceremoniously deposited in Chatfield Forest.

"Some living memory," I say as Sloan gently grasps my elbow and helps me to my feet.

"It's not an exact science," he says and I feel ashamed of my remark, considering the fact that Finn could even create something that could get us this close to home is a miracle in and of itself.

The twin moons are high in the sky, softening the red glare of the never-setting sun and casting everything in a rosy pink hue. At the edge of the forest, the trees are sparse and you can see the dim lights of the colony. There used to be so many, but now I stand between the trees and watch as lights periodically blink out. We have the Metal stone now, but that's only a small piece to the larger puzzle. I have to figure out how to destroy it.

Meanwhile, there's still the disease that incubated in Ahna, and that's now festering inside how many unknowing colonists? And then there's the Citizen Law Enforcement, blindly acting on behalf of the Imminent Darkness. Oh, and don't forget the Leadership Council. Who knows where their loyalties truly lie, even though I have my suspicions, all my evidence is circumstantial at best. Not to mention the actual Imminent Darkness.

I let out an unintentional sigh, and when I do something strange happens. A vision superimposes over the silhouette of stone, glass, and wooden buildings in the distance. I see nothing but barren red land stretched for kilometers, a large scarlet belly of a sun hanging in the blood sky. Then I watch as space ships land, men and women

216

spilling out of them. It's like watching a time lapsed movie. Buildings are built and blurs of people move about. The buildings change with the passage of time, but only slightly. The twin moons rise and set, rise and set. There's a consistent ebb and flow. But then it seems to slow. The busyness of the colony seems to dissipate. Where there were once thousands of tiny pinpricks of light, now there is maybe only a single thousand. I watch as the lights slowly blink out. A darkness seems to encapsulate the colony, surrounding it in a black fog, but none of its inhabitants seem to notice as they go about their daily affairs.

Is this what the Imminent Darkness has done to us? All this time, and no one the wiser. Until now. More lights extinguish. Blurred figures in long, hooded cloaks. The darkness grows denser until it surrounds our small colony and obscures my view. The black so thick, palpable as if I could reach out and touch it.

"Ka."

Sloan's voice is soft as I feel his fingers tighten in the crook of my elbow. He sounds far away, but I slowly turn my head and blink. His angular face coming back into focus.

It wasn't real. None of it was real. It was simply the passage of time. My Elemental gift from Constancia, the goddess of Wood. Is it a coincidence that this vision was the result of a gift from the same Element that makes up our Leadership Council?

"Are you okay?" His fingers slide up my arm and over my shoulder to find my cheek. I close my eyes against his warmth and nod. When I open them again, his piercing green eyes are searching mine for reassurance. For truth.

I place my hand over his. "It was just a vision."

It feels like a lie on my tongue. I told myself it wasn't real, but is seeing in the moment what makes something real? My father told me once that the future isn't stagnant, it can be changed. Rewritten. Our choices shape our future, for better or worse, we are the ones in charge of our destiny. If I believe in—if I choose—a different future, then is the one that I saw a lie? My stomach clenches at the thought.

"I hate to break up whatever this is," Cerise whispers from behind me. "But I really think that we should get back to the tent city." There's a strange lilt to her voice and when I turn, she has her hand on the hilt of her dagger, ready to yank it from the folds of her hair. Her hazel eyes dart around the forest, a slight curl to her upper lip.

I shake my head, snapping myself out of the remnants of the vision.

"Cerise?" Li asks.

I follow Cerise's darting glances and then I see it. The forest around us seems to be moving, as if the shadows are breathing. Alive. The Imminent Darkness is here.

"If we go, we lead it to the others," Sloan says voicing my immediate concern.

"What do we do?" Doran asks. There doesn't seem to be any order to the movements. Shadows dance in and out from in between the trees, their forms writhing and undefined. I've only seen the Imminent Darkness take the form of something living. A mummy. A wolf. A little girl. A codger. I've never seen it take the form of something that is essentially formless.

"I don't think it's the Imminent Darkness," I say watching as the same dancing pattern of shadows plays out again. The exact same ebb and flow over and over again.

"How do you know?" Cerise challenges, her muscles taut ready for another fight.

"Watch the shadows. They don't change. They're repeating the same patterns over and over again. And the Imminent Darkness is energy, it needs a form. Shadows don't have a form. I think it's something else."

Cerise doesn't budge. I give Sloan a meaningful glance and I see his shoulders dip in resignation. His highly logical brain doesn't agree with me, but he's giving in anyways. Trusting my judgment. I head down the unmarked path, silvery leaves crunching beneath my boots as I head toward the hidden entrance to the tent city.

Li puts a hand on Cerise's shoulder and she sighs deeply, sheathing her dagger. They fall into step behind us, Cerise casting one final menacing glare at the shadows.

"What do you think it is, if not the ID?" Doran asks in a low voice.

"I'm not sure I know. But I bet we can find someone who does."

. . .

Finn turns the cool, hematite fragment over in his palm. His eyes are unseeing, but the corners of his mouth twitch as he uses his knobby fingers to inspect every centimeter of its surface. Doran has gone to get treated for his bruised ribs. Li and Cerise lean against the table anxiously. Cerise drums her fingers nervously on the table's surface. I know that she didn't trust my judgment in the forest earlier, and if I'm being honest, my feelings are slightly hurt by it. I mean, I got us out of the Isle of Tonitrui without any of our blood being shed, a little trust would go a long way. But I know that trust doesn't come easily to someone who lived under the Water Queen's rule, so I bite my tongue.

Sloan's shoulder is pressed against mine. His Water markings may be gone, but his personality still contains the calm, gentleness that comes with his lost Elemental affiliation. The serenity to my storm. Because if I am right about the shadows, that's what's coming. A storm.

"Someone hand me the Visometer," Finn finally says. Sloan jumps to attention and grabs a strange looking device from the haphazard shelving on the wall behind a workbench. He places it on the table. It has a small, steel platform that looks like a scale on top of a rectangular base. Two sets of wires run from either side of the device, attached to a diode.

Finn takes the Metal stone and carefully places it onto the platform. He then takes a wire in either hand and prepares to touch them to the stone.

"What's that thing do?" asks Li, leaning on his elbows and peering wearily over his clasped hands.

"This thing is called a Visometer. It measures the energy of matter. Well, actually, it can only measure two of three states of matter. Solid and liquid. In this case, a solid. I just take either of these diodes and press it to the stone. Then it will give me a reading on the output of energy being given off."

Finn presses the wires to the gray surface. Instantly, the lights from the underground generators flicker momentarily, casting us in a moment of darkness, before stabilizing and coming back on. The stone crackles and crooked, white lines of electricity form a protective halo around the stone, Finn gasps, jerking the wires away, but the stone still buzzes with the current.

Finn licks his cracked lips. The tips of his fingers are singed black from the power of the Metal stone. "I guess the obvious thing to say would be that indeed, this stone of yours carries a substantial amount of energy inside it." The stone hisses in response.

"The Land of Metal was strange. There was a lot of lightning and thunder. Even the inhabitants seemed electrically charged," Sloan says.

"You could feel it. Like a constant buzzing in your ears," Cerise adds.

"Interesting." Finn cautiously sets the wires down onto the table, careful to leave the stone untouched for now. The protective halo has dissipated, but the stone still seems to buzz with energy. "If what you say is accurate, then my impression is that the Metal stone is not simply a stone that was used to harbor part of your fractured personality. This stone is much more powerful than that."

"How powerful?" Li asks, finally regaining some interest.

"Well. That depends on several factors. Some of which are

unknown. We don't know what else was done to the stone. Yes, we know that originally the stone was a gift and that later a protective charm was used and it was tossed back into the Elemental Abyss. But what about after it was tossed into the Abyss? We've no idea what happened to it then. Whose possession did you say the stone was in?"

"I'm not sure they actually possessed it, but Isa said the Chief Tonitrui knew where it was kept."

"The Chief Tonitrui and Isa didn't seem to get along," Sloan jumps in. "The Chief knew exactly how to get us to the stone, although I'm fairly certain he thought we would die trying to retrieve it."

"And what kind of people were the Tonitrui?" Finn prompts. He folds his arms across his chest, brow furrowed like a bushy, white caterpillar across his forehead.

"They were almost like giants made of stone. All the vegetation was made of the same gray gemstone and when the Tonitrui spoke it was a roar like thunder," Cerise describes, hazel eyes wide at the memory. "It was as if they were the thunder itself."

Something dawns on me then and I feel so stupid for not having noticed it sooner. "And Isa's servants, like Oosa and Aama. The Fulgurs. Their bodies seemed to spark with lightning. It was visible on their skin."

"People made of thunder and lightning," Li says. He glances across the table at me with a wry smile. "I'd say I'm surprised, but I think I'm past that emotion these days."

"And you said Isa—with her servants made of lightning—and these thunder people didn't get along?" Finn asks, pressing his lips together. His unseeing eyes linger on the Metal stone which still rests cradled on the device's platform.

"They didn't seem to. Isa called the Tonitrui tricksters. And they lived in a land across the sea, two and a half days' time by air ship. I'm not sure if by choice or by force," I reply.

Finn's expression has made me anxious. I had thought the stones belonged to me. But just because something belongs to you doesn't mean that other people can't try and use it for their own means. A long silence stretches across the table before Finn finally speaks again.

"I think that it is good you retrieved the stone. Its power is palpable. Metal. It's not like the other Elements. It's different. It's stronger than any of the others, but it's also cunning. It is near impossible to inject a person with the Metal Element and maintain Balance. Those who pronounce it, pronounce almost certain outcast from their family and friends. But do you know the reason that Metal becomes so easily Unbalanced?"

I shake my head, then remember his blindness and my manners. "No." Finn's eyes find me across the table, the silver threads spread across his cheek and up to his forehead like the webbing of a spider.

"It is because Metal is very powerful, just like this stone, each of us buzzes with it." He holds up his singed fingertips. "This stone contains an enormous amount of power. Essentially, this stone is a crystal and crystals have been used for thousands of years to transmit energy. It can take energy in one state and convert it into another state. From the feel of it, this stone is hematite, as you described. Hematite is a grounding stone with magnetic properties. And yet, we see that it can produce an electrical current of some kind."

"Like lightning?" Li asks.

"Yes, like lightning. For the sake of explanation, the Imminent Darkness is potential energy. The Universe needs balance in order to exist. Everything consists of matter and matter contains energy. Matter's opposite is dark matter. Energy's opposite is the same: dark energy. That is the biology of the Imminent Darkness on a chemical level." Finn picks up the stone which has finally stopped cackling and resumed its normal appearance. "This stone contains that dark energy. Essentially, it has the capabilities to convert one energy type into another and back again. Whoever possessed this stone would hold great power. I have a feeling your aunt didn't want you to retrieve this stone solely for your own gain."

So, I was right. Sort of. Isa wanted the stone. But then who set fire to our fuel containers? Despite her all night raving, maybe the Fulgurs didn't want someone like Isa—someone flippant, childish, and careless—to have this kind of power. Maybe the Tonitrui were a safer option. Thunder and lightning. You can't have one without the other.

I ask the remaining question that's been gnawing at my mind. "What kind of power would the stone have given Isa?"

Finn smiles grimly. "My girl, this stone contains the power to control the Imminent Darkness. If the energy of the Imminent

Darkness can be changed from one form to another, it can be manipulated, controlled, even destroyed. The energy inside this stone can change worlds. That's what was causing the shadows you saw in the forest. It was a residual effect of the Land of Metal. The energy brought with you from your travels had nowhere else to go, so it was locked in a kind of energetic loop. For all we know, it still could be. Maybe even forever. But, here I am, talking in circles."

He holds up the stone.

"This is the reason Metal Elementals become Unbalanced so easily, the dark energy has nowhere else to go. Everyone's chemical makeup is unique. For most Elementals this poses no problem, as the light and dark energies easily find balance. But this isn't so for the Metal Elemental. The substance used to induce the physiological changes that we bear creates a sort of anomaly. The Metal Element contains electromagnetic energy that throws the balance of light and dark off kilter. The result is a constant battle being waged inside each Metal Elemental, most of the time completely unbeknownst to them. This is the secret of Metal."

"So, wait. What you're saying, is that Metals are feared and ridiculed for being Unblanaced, and it's because of something that we do to our *own* people?" Li sounds both shocked and horrified.

"But why?" Cerise asks. "I don't understand."

"Metal has many strong components. If the energies can stay balanced, then a Metal Elemental is a force to be reckoned with. They are some of our strongest bodies and brightest minds."

What he says rings true. I think of Mrs. Chatfield and Zora. Finn himself. Bina. Bax. I have yet to meet a Metal, besides Michaela, who has been unkind to me. But let's be honest, the girl isn't quite as balanced as she may think. Perhaps her dark energy is winning the battle that rages inside of her. And it's no fault of her own. She can't help but be what she was engineered to be.

"But the war going on inside of them. Inside of me," Finn gestures at his own chest. "It's a ticking time bomb."

Sloan interrupts. "But it doesn't have to be this way. Not anymore, does it?"

Finn nods, handing me the stone. It's cold and heavy in my palm, like he just relieved himself of a weighty burden. "This stone has the power not to just rid us of the Imminent Darkness, but to change everything. It has the power to change *us*."

CHAPTER 20

It's quiet in the tent, save for the soft murmurs of Li and Cerise in the opposite corner and the slow even lilt of Sloan's breath beside me. My body is exhausted but my mind is reeling from the events of the last few days.

The revelation that the Metal stone could not only restore my powers—my so-called gifts—back to me, but also change the energetic makeup of every Metal Elemental puts an inordinate amount of pressure on me to destroy it. Sloan's arm is slung across my stomach, but my hands are free and I turn the cool hematite over in my fingers in the dim light of the single lantern. It looks innocuous enough. But it explains why Isa may have wanted me to retrieve it. She thought that I would bring it back to her. Only the Fulgurs knew better. Somehow they were acting in alliance with the Tonitrui. If not in alliance, then at least in solidarity. A stone powerful enough to change the energetic makeup of a being. Should anyone have that much power? Should I?

Sloan sighs in his sleep. I slip the stone back into the front pocket of my jeans and turn into him so that I am curled against his chest. His breath is warm on my forehead. The Elemental stones are supposed to help me defeat the Imminent Darkness. But it would seem with each retrieval comes a price. Everly's death and Li's scars with the Fire stone, my mother's near death and father's disappearance with the Earth stone. My own almost drowning and Li's dance with darkness because of the Wood stone. Sloan's curse and loss of his Water upon retrieving the Water stone. Each one carries with it an unspoken burden. What burden does the Metal stone bring with it?

My mind drifts to the only remaining item in the tiny burlap sack Bina gave to me, which now seems so long ago. A perfect, clear crystal. Finn explained that crystals have energetic properties and the ability to transform energy from one type to another. Physical to chemical. Light to dark. What will happen to the Metal Elementals— to Finn, Bina, Zora, Mrs. Chatfield, Bax—and I cringe to say it— even Michaela—what will happen to them if I destroy the Metal stone? But I have to destroy it. Bina has made that very clear since the beginning. In order to restore that piece of me—the strong, courageous part that is associated with Metal—I will need to destroy it. In theory, the change—if any—should be a positive one. The dark energy that causes a Metal to become so easily Unbalanced *should* be converted to light energy. But that too comes with a price. Will it change who they are at their very core?

Maybe someone like Michaela isn't meant to be all sugary roses. Maybe she's meant to have a darkness to her. If that's what makes her, well, *her*. And who am I to change that? As much as I might think she's a witchy, traitorous brat, it doesn't give me the right to change that. I sigh and Sloan instinctively wraps his arm tighter around me, pulling me in closer. Others have had to change without a choice. Don't we all—at one point or another—have to change and not necessarily have a say in the matter? I didn't ask to be the Impossible Girl of Legend. None of us did.

The Imminent Darkness needs to be stopped. Before the disease that took Ahna's life can spread throughout the colony and take even more innocent lives. I curl in closer to Sloan, my eyelids finally growing heavy with the weight of sleep that gnaws at the edges of my mind. I have to destroy the stone to stop it. Or do I?

...

Sloan paces the dirt floor of the meeting tent. He's been more on edge and mumbling in his sleep. With his ability to dream walk I don't know where he's been or what he's seen. Or maybe they're just simply regular dreams. For now, he's kept me in the dark. But I suspect when it matters most is when he will tell me and not a moment too soon. Since the beginning Sloan has been big on making sure he doesn't interfere with my choices. Even though Bina saw me entering into their lives and Sloan's willingness to take an Everlasting Vow that binds our fates, he has always made it clear that my choices are mine and mine alone.

The tent is taken up by a long, narrow table adorned with an array of gadgets and devices. Mrs. Chatfield sits at it, a serene pool of energy in contrast to Sloan's frenetic pacing. I lean over the table and inspect some of the items more closely. It looks like something Li would have procured: cloaking devices, two-way transmitters, message tubes, a transmission disrupter, and a plethora of other things I couldn't even begin to name. If I didn't know better, I'd say it looks like someone raided the military complex. Maybe they did. Then it dawns on me. Not they. He. Bax.

As I think his name, he enters the tent. His blue eyes are in cool contrast to his fiery hair. His t-shirt stretches across his muscular frame and he has a bruise on his angular jaw where a week's worth of stubble graces his chin. No longer the Wood Council's soldier. How easily some of us slip into other roles. Zechariah enters behind him, pulling the ties to let loose the entrance's flaps so that they fall closed behind him.

There's the tactile meeting room, a small cavern off one of the many tunnels beneath Chatfield Forest, but this meeting is closed doors. Zechariah's face is drawn and his eyes tired. Sloan stops pacing when they enter and gives each man a brotherly pat on the back.

"Have you told them?" Zechariah asks Chanice. Her hands are wrapped around a sloppily constructed clay mug.

"No. I was waiting for you. You are the leader here." But we all know the truth. Zechariah is leader in name only. Mrs. Chatfield is as much the leader of the tent city as he is, with her healing hands, various tinctures, and kind words.

"Please, sit." Zechariah spreads his leathery hands wide indicating the empty chairs around the table. The words are less a gesture of politeness than a command. "We have word from the colony. New refugees arrived last eve." Refugees. That's what the tent city has become. A safe haven from the brutality of the Imminent Darkness and the Leadership Council's lack of interest in stopping it.

"How many?" Sloan asks.

"Twenty," Mrs. Chatfield replies softly.

"Twenty at once? But that's never happened before!" I exclaim. At first it was mainly the Metals, those in the Underground who knew Mrs. Chatfield, that followed her to the safety of the tent city. But gradually, people of all Elements have made their way here. Seeking protection or training or help.

"And seventeen more this morning," Zechariah adds grimly. My head is spinning. The caverns already seemed full to capacity before, and upon our return we had all shared tents willingly, but I hadn't stopped to think about why. Where could all these people go? The colony isn't all that big to begin with. Surely, the Council will take notice of all the empty homes. People not showing up to their jobs.

"But why so many, so quickly?" I ask rubbing my hands back and forth over the worn, salvaged wood that was used to make the table. Zechariah glances at Chanice and she tilts her head to the side and purses her lips as if she's about to deliver news that I'd probably wish I wouldn't be hearing.

"They are calling it the *cassusmortem*." I shake my head, not recognizing the term. But Sloan's face has gone pale.

"The empty death," he whispers.

"Yes. It is the disease you spoke of. From the tiny insects. One of the thirty-seven new refugees is a doctor. He said the hospital is full to capacity and there aren't enough staff to take care of the influx of patients. Businesses are closed. People are staying home, either too ill or too afraid to leave."

My stomach clenches in a knot. I remember the swarm hatching out of Ahna's lifeless body and heading toward the colony. Toward my home. Or at least what was left of it.

"The disease it would seem, devours one from the inside out. First, affecting the nervous system. It mimics insanity—making the person say and do things that are out of character—before slowly shutting down their organs one by one," Mrs. Chatfield explains. And for the first time I notice the sag of her shoulders, what the weight of this knowledge has done to her.

"Because making them say and do cruel things to those they love and who would help them isn't enough? It has to be slow and painful on top of it?" Bax spits disgusted. Is this why he went and got all of these gadgets and devices? What family does he still have alive who haven't made it to safety? Does he even know if they're still alive?

"That is why they call it the empty death. The ones you love are nothing but a shell of who they once were when death finally comes for them," Zechariah doesn't hide the disgust from his voice.

Ahna's bloody lips and dark, hollowed eyes. She was nothing but the shell of my best friend. Once brilliant and vibrant, with lustrous black hair and gorgeous tawny skin. Beautiful, intelligent, loving, and determined. Determined to help me and then determined to save her twin. I feel the surge of anger in my blood, but I'm not quick enough to pull my fingers away before I singe the table top, black fingerprints where my hands once were. I clasp my hands together and drop them into my lap.

"And what about the Council? What are they doing to help? Have they set up makeshift hospitals? Have the military started working on some kind of antidote?" I ask.

Mrs. Chatfield clears her throat. "That's the peculiar thing. The Council is some of the first that were affected with the *cassusmortem*. Four of the five members were among the first dead."

My head flings up. But how is that possible? I was so sure that the Imminent Darkness and the Council of Leaders were somehow in this together. I didn't know how, but I saw the proof for myself. The prisoners kept below Council Hall, the creepy statue of the codger…Sloan glances at me with a raised eyebrow. Not condescending, but a reminder that there could still be hope.

"The only Council member to survive is Esmeralda. But she is not in very good condition, from what I've heard." The sole female of the Leadership Council.

"But then who's in charge?" Bax asks.

"The Citizen Law Enforcement has taken over Council Hall." Zechariah states it simply as fact, but I can hear the underlying fear in his voice.

"That's impossible…" Sloan begins, but Mrs. Chatfield gently cuts him off.

"Five leaders, Sloan. No one thought, that in a place that has seen such prolonged peace, that all five leaders would be dead or incapacitated at the same time. The safety was supposed to be in the numbers. But that's changed now." She turns to me, grabbing my hand. Her dark brown eyes are fierce when she says, "That's why we can no longer wait, Ka. It's only a matter of time before someone brings the *cassusmortem* to the tent city, if someone hasn't already. The Imminent Darkness needs defeated."

"But—I—" I want to say that I'm not ready or that I don't know how. But I am as ready as I will ever be. I look at each of their faces. The yearning behind Bax's baby blues, the intensity of Zechariah's tired gaze, the hope in Mrs. Chatfield's warm brown eyes, and the trust in Sloan's sea green ones. "But I don't have a plan."

There's a rustling at the entrance to the tent. Bax leaps up, hand instinctively going to his hip where his gun would usually be holstered, but his fingers grasp at air.

An old woman with frizzy gray hair and sharp gray eyes enters the tent. She isn't very tall, but her shoulders are thrown back and she wears a shapeless, black dress like it's something made of the finest silks and furs. She smiles, revealing several empty gaps.

"Yeh may not have a plan, Kata. But I most certainly do."

CHAPTER 21

"Bina!" Zora and Doran carefully guide Sloan's mother into the tent and over toward the table. Sloan helps her sit down, taking the knobby cane with which she now walks, thanks to the Imminent Darkness. The Imminent Darkness feeds on negative energy and the Citizen Law Enforcement is full of it. The effects of their MindCleanse attempt have aged Bina rapidly. Couple that with a difficult life without her husband (not to mention a psychopathic daughter) and Bina looks much older than her sixty-something years.

"But Mom. How?" Sloan asks. He drapes a protective arm across her shoulders and his brow is furrowed.

"Now, now. None of that, Son." Bina gently pats his hand which grasps her bony shoulder. She smells of smoke and herbs. Was she creating some kind of concoction or tincture before she came here?

"That big oaf there—" She points a spindle-finger at Bax and a pink flush creeps across his cheeks, but he smiles. Sloan had said Bax was a long-time friend, of course Bina would have known him too. "And the lovely Zora fetched me."

"What about Michaela?" I ask, even though part of me fears her discovering my location. I can't imagine sparing her life suddenly made her all rainbows and butterflies. To her I am still Most Wanted Person Number One. Not to mention who else could be looking for me since my escape. But people are dying. Our colony's lone hospital is filled to capacity. Surely, that takes precedence over a teenage girl.

Bina gives me a tight smile. "She's on a mandatory leave of absence. After yer escape, and subsequent sparing of her life, she was seen as unfit for duty. For now, she stays in the military complex. It kills her though. Sitting. Watching. Waiting. That is not the thread from which my daughter has been cut." Bina reaches across the table and pats my hand. "Don't ye worry about her, Ka. I don't think she'll be bothering ye none."

Sloan still looks bamboozled by his mother's presence. "Does Dad know that you're here?"

"Of course, my boy. Sit. Yer making my nerves unravel." Sloan immediately obeys and slumps into a chair beside his mother. "Now, I wasn't brought here for idle chitchat. We have to discuss the sickness."

"The *cassusmortem*," Doran supplies. He's leaning on the table between his own mother and Zechariah, fiddling with one of the gadgets strewn across its surface.

"Yes, yes. The empty death. Unnecessarily morbid name if yeh ask me." Bina turns to me. "Yeh have the Metal stone?" She holds her hand out expectantly and I drop it into her wrinkled palm. She closes her eyes and takes a slow breath, most likely feeling the strange energy that it emits. "It's as I thought." She hands it back to me. It's not even warm from being in someone's hand; it remains cool as ice.

"What do you think, Bina?" asks Zechariah. His hands are clasped beneath his chin, elbows resting on the table. He leans forward, curiosity etched on his face.

"Do ye still have the bag I gave yeh long ago?"

I nod, fishing in my messenger bag for the small, burlap sack. I pull it out and empty the single remaining item onto the table: the crystal. It shimmers in the dim light of the lanterns. It looks perfect, like a star fallen from the sky. It's all crisp angles and shimmering surfaces, wide at one end then converging to a sharp, pointed tip.

Bina picks it up and inspects it, closing one gray eye. She places it back on the table in front of me.

"The sickness, the *cassusmortem* as yeh call it, is killing our colony. Soon there may be nothing left. If the illness travels into the tent city, then there isn't much left we can do. I've been working on some medicines, but they aren't a cure. They can't put off the inevitable."

Zora clears her throat. She stares at the table. "It's already here. The last group of refugees. It's already starting. The sallow skin and sunken in eyes. We have them quarantined in a separate cavern, but, Bina, we all breathe the same air down here. I'm afraid time is running out."

237

My heart sinks into my stomach. The sickness is here. *Cassusmortem*. The empty death. I'm not sure I could bear to watch another person I love suffer the same fate as Ahna. Mrs. Chatfield glances up and catches my paled expression.

"We're doing the best we can," she whispers. Zechariah puts a reassuring hand onto her shoulder.

"We all are, Chanice. Bina's remedy will help. For now. It will buy them—us—more time."

"The sickness isn't all," Bina continues. "The Council is all but absolved. Only Esmeralda remains and she is quite ill. The Citizen Law Enforcement—the human minions of the Imminent Darkness—have taken over. Any colonists who aren't afflicted with *cassusmortem* have taken to their homes. Their numbers are dwindling. Their loved ones are dying. They're afraid. And we both know how the Imminent Darkness feels about fear."

I nod, swallowing the lump in my throat. "It feeds on it. It makes it stronger."

Bina gives me an approving nod.

"It intended for this to happen all along," Doran's lip curls in anger. "Did we ever stand a chance?" Zora gives her little brother a meaningful look and he averts his eyes back to the cloaking device in his hands.

"We do stand a chance. But it isn't going to be easy. Chanice, the most recent batch of the tincture is in my tent. Finn can help yeh distribute it. Don't forget to wear yer masks. Zechariah, I'm going to need a list of all the refugees in the tent city. Doran, Bax and Zora,

238

tally the weapons in the arsenal. We may need to take arms soon. And Son, go make me a cup of tea. Be sure it's extra hot."

Everyone stares at Bina for a beat, then scrambles into action. Her presence, Seer or not, carries with it a certain amount of authority that seems almost otherworldly. Although she appears fragile and now has to use a cane, there's no doubt in my mind that she could bring an army to its knees.

Once the tent flap closes behind the last person to leave, Bina turns to me. She grasps my hand and I'm transported to the first time we met. When she was a Seer in the Black Bazaar and she told me my future. A future I thought was impossible. But turns out is very, very possible. But this time her eyes don't roll back into her head and there are no ominous predictions.

"My dear, girl. Yeh are so very brave." Bina strokes my hand with her long, bony fingers. When she looks back up at me, her eyes are glassy with tears. "And I am so very sorry."

There is no shimmer to her features. No lie to be revealed by my Water gift. I gulp down my fright and try to summon some courage. "Am I going to die?" I ask softly.

Bina tilts her head. "That remains to be seen." No shimmer. I feel my shoulders relax. "But even so, yeh will have a burden to bear. It is my job to make sure yeh are prepared to make it."

"A choice?" That's not exactly what I was steeling myself for.

Bina releases my hand and takes the Metal stone. She places it carefully beside the crystal. The stone easily dwarfs the crystal in size. "Finn told me yeh understand that crystals can transform energy,

239

yes?" I nod. More or less. "Well, that's not all they can do when magic is involved."

My pulse begins to quicken. She points to the Metal stone. "Yeh know that ye are meant to destroy the Metal stone. Ye know that it is very powerful and has the potential to change many things. If ye destroy the Metal stone, the final piece to yer fractured self will be returned to yeh. Just like the others. But—" Why must there always be a *but?*—"Destroying it will change the energetic make up of every single Metal that still lives. Michaela, myself, Finn. Bax, Zora, Chanice."

I clear my throat. "I thought that it might make you Balanced."

Bina smiles at me, a pitying smile. "Dear girl, whoever said I wasn't Balanced?" She points to the Metal stone. "Sloan mentioned what happened with yer fire in the Land of Metal. Yer Fire energy flared when it met with the Metal energy. Scared him a bit, it did. But destroying that stone will give yeh all yer Elemental powers. With those powers yeh can defeat the Imminent Darkness."

Well, that explains why Sloan lied. He probably didn't understand what had happened. I'm not sure I totally do myself. But somehow this all seems too simple. Nothing can ever be that simple. At least not when it comes to me. "What about the crystal?"

She moves her knobby finger to the crystal. I notice the thin, tarnished silver band around her ring finger. Her wedding band. Finn. Brilliant, valiant Finn. Who am I to change that?

"If ye destroy the crystal, yer Metal will not be returned to yeh and the Metal Elemental energy will not be transformed. The destruction of the crystal will close the Elemental Abyss. Forever."

My head jerks up, eyes searching her face. I have to admit, one of the things I admire about Bina is that she does not look away. Even when she is revealing a difficult truth, her gaze remains steadfast.

"My parents." I run my thumb over the turquoise ring on my index finger. Bina's eyes drift to the ring Doran created out of a fragment of the Earth stone. My mother's stone.

"Unfortunately, it will not work. Once the Elemental Abyss is gone, the magic is gone with it. Xon 9 will be closed off from the other lands for good. No more objects of living memory. The Imminent Darkness included. The Elemental Abyss has a large energetic pull. It drew the Imminent Darkness here. You are part of that pull."

"Will destroying the crystal kill me too then?" The backs of my eyes burn. I feel like I'm in one of my dreams where I'm lost in a vast ocean, with no land in sight. Saltwater burning my lungs. Gasping for air. In this moment I am drowning on land.

Bina gives me a hard look. "I cannot see it."

"But. But you can see everything! You're a seer!"

There's a hysterical edge to my voice. I take a deep breath, trying to calm myself down. What difference does it make? No man knows when death will come to knock on his door. Why should I be any different? Half-immortal or not. I'm still half-mortal, as Sloan likes to point out. I cast my eyes down in shame. "I'm sorry."

"Nonsense, Child. I cannot see it because it is not a fixed point. The decision yeh make…it will alter the fabric of our reality. Of the

Universe itself." She gives my hand a consoling pat.

"You knew all this time? About the crystal? What it could do?" I ask. The old me—the me from before—would have been angry, felt betrayed.

"I had an idea. But when it comes to these things, one can never be sure." She holds my gaze, but there's a softening of her features. A gentle blurring. Like looking into the ripples of a puddle. A lie.

"If I destroy the Metal stone, I get my gift, but change the energetic make up of every single Metal Elemental in the entire colony. But will it destroy the Imminent Darkness?"

"It will weaken it greatly."

"But it's not a guarantee?"

She shakes her head, a curly gray strand falling across her angular cheek. I never noticed how much of Sloan I can see in his mother's face. If I look carefully, I can almost see what Bina looked like when she was younger, less tired. Less burdened with the weight of the Impossible Girl and sacrificing her livelihood to defeating the Imminent Darkness and its stronghold on her family.

"Nothing is ever a guarantee. But the only way to truly rid our planet of the Imminent Darkness is to destroy the Elemental Abyss."

I take a deep, shaky breath. "So choice two. Destroy the crystal, destroy the Elemental Abyss. The Metal Elementals stay as they are. I never see my parents again. And I may or may not die. Okay, then. So, yeah. Well." A nervous laugh escapes my lips and I gulp.

Bina gives me a sad look. "I know it isn't an easy choice, Ka. But I know that yeh will make the best choice."

242

I notice that she doesn't use the word *right*. Neither choice is right nor wrong. Not really. She picks up her cane and leans over to give me a hug. Before she pulls away, she whispers softly in my ear. "The choice may seem impossible, but we both know that the truth is never impossible."

CHAPTER 22

Once I'm alone, I snatch one of the cloaking cuffs off the table. I slide it over my wrist and carefully slide the button located on its underside, knowing that it will render me invisible to the naked eye. Some high-tech science stuff about wavelengths and perception.

I peek out the tent flap to make sure no one is loitering around outside, but everyone is still off tending to Bina's wishes. Slipping out, I let the tent flap close behind me. I make my way down one of the countless rows of tents, heading toward the wooden stairs that leads back to the surface and into Chatfield Forest.

People are huddled together in small groups. Children are playing with dirty stuffed animals and wooden blocks. Simple toys. Toys that were easy to take if you were disappearing. Everyone talks in hushed tones. Some adults practice their trade: whittling wood or shaping metal. One tent has a small table outside its entrance with rows of small cups filled with soil. There's a portable lamp clamped to the table's surface. Most likely an Earth Elemental doing what they do best—making things grow and thrive.

I walk past the intake area where a brief medical exam is performed and refugees with the beginning signs of *cassusmortem* are quarantined. I pass the training area, the clink of metal on metal ringing in my ears. I continue unnoticed, catching snippets of conversation about the Imminent Darkness, Esmeralda, and the *cassusmortem*. Once, I even catch the words Impossible Girl. But then I hear the word *dream* uttered in the same breath.

If only this were all a bad dream, if I was dream walking like Sloan, Bina, or my mother and could wake up any second back in my bed. Back in my room at home with the pink light filtering through the sheer curtains. My mother sitting on the bed beside me, brushing the hair off my forehead. Maybe it would even be before Pronouncement. Before any of this was even set into motion.

I'm lost in thought as I make my way to the stairs, so I fail to notice when someone blocks my path. I walk right into a sturdy chest and tumble backward, but not before the same someone grips my wrists. How is that possible, when no one can see me?

"I told you. I always see you," says a gruff voice. I look up into chocolate brown, almond-shaped eyes flanked by long, dark lashes. Li. For the first time in a while, it's as if I'm really seeing him.

We haven't been this close in some time. His hair has grown out, curling around his ears and draping into his eyes. He's filled out from all the training he's been doing, and although I know he has no intention of hurting me, his grip is like iron shackles around my wrists. What if someone saw him grasping at the air? But there's no one else around.

"How?" I ask, searching his face. There's a cut beneath his eye and the yellow remnants of a bruise on his cheek, the one without the black tattooed swirls of Fire.

"Well, I suppose when I first said that, it was a bit of a fib." I remember the first time I used the cloaking cuff and how, even though I was invisible, he reached out and kissed me. That was a long time ago. A lifetime ago. "I can actually smell you. When you walked past the training area. You always smell like flowery soap, grass, and something else that I could never place. But then, after going to the Land of Metal, I realized what it was. It's the sea. You smell like the salty, ocean air. For as long as I can remember. Which is strange, considering there's no water around here."

"Strange," I mumble. Is it because my mother is an Earth? Or my connection to Sloan? I shake my head. It doesn't really matter.

Li's grip loosens around my wrists. "I figured you could use some company." His expression softens.

"You don't even know where I'm going," I reply.

He grins. "Obviously, you're going above ground. And you're doing it with a cloaking cuff, so my guess is that you don't want anyone to know that you're doing that. Sounds dangerous to me. Danger is my middle name."

"I'm pretty sure your middle name is Alexander."

"Either way. You don't have to do this alone, Ka. Whatever it is that Bina or anyone else told you. You're not some martyr." His smile vanishes. His hands drop from my wrists, shoved bashfully into the pocket of his hoodie. "You're my best friend. The only one I have left." My heart slows at his words. He's not the only one with an Ahna-shaped size hole in his heart. But they were twins. I can't begin to understand the depths of his grief. Now, I know maybe a little why Ahna was so furious with me whenever her brother's life rested in my hands. Some connections are irreplaceable.

"I think you're right. Some company is just what I need," I relent.

Any semblance of sadness disappears from his features, replaced by a mischievous sparkle in his eyes. He grins, flipping up his hood.

"Then let's get going."

. . .

The first thing that I notice is the darkness. The twin moons are beginning to rise, casting everything in a pink tint, and yet the darkness seems to creep all around us. Chatfield Forest is past the perimeter of the colony. The hair on the back of my neck rises as we pass the military complex, edging our way past Pax Park where Li was attacked and nearly died. This part of the colony holds so many bad memories.

To anyone passing us Li would just appear to be a guy going for a walk, hands shoved into the pocket of his hoodie, hood pulled up over his jet-black hair. They wouldn't see me, my shoulder pressed against his, our steps walking in matching rhythm.

Li takes a left bypassing the Underground, and heading toward

Sloan's neighborhood of round, stone houses. Council Hall, the University complex, and the hospital are all on the opposite side of the colony.

There's a rustle from a silvery-green cluster of bushes and I nearly jump out of my skin, clutching Li's arm, his bicep tense beneath my fingers. But it's only some trash, tumbling through thanks to the ever-constant breeze the planet offers.

Maybe this wasn't such a good idea. I'm thankful for Li's presence, and thankful that I wasn't stubborn enough to insist that I come alone. I may have magical powers, but it doesn't mean that I'm invincible. Nor does it mean that I'm not afraid.

The small bungalows cast shadows that seem to ebb and flow with a life of their own. Street lights remain unlit. Most of the houses are dark. We pass the top of Sloan's street and keep going, cutting an angle that will take us right in between Council Hall and the school. The school is L-shaped, with the lower school being attached to the main building. The colony is small, only about three-thousand people—at least it was small, probably even smaller now with the *cassusmortem*. There were strict rules to avoid overpopulation and hunger, two of the main points of suffering on Old Earth.

Li's pace is quick and I can tell that he's just as uncomfortable as I am at being here. There is no one around, no one out and about. No one running errands. No one walking to or from work. Every now and then there will be a dim light in one of the windows we pass of a house or business. But otherwise, it's eerily silent. As if everyone just got up and disappeared. I suppose they almost have.

The hair on the back of my neck prickles and I don't let go of the crook of Li's elbow. I think he needs reminded of my presence as much as I need reminded of his. I turn to my right as we pass Council Hall. My stomach lurches. There are hand-painted wooden signs scattered about the ground around the fountain of the codger. Some are broken in half. A dirty jacket lays in a heap and there's a single shoe.

"There were protests. I heard the refugees talking about them," Li mumbles, even though no one else is around to hear us.

"What happened to them?"

He shrugs. "No one seemed to know."

We continue walking, the glass and steel of Council Hall gleaming menacingly in the moonlight. I can think of a few things that may have happened. Kidnapping. MindCleanse. Murder. Imprisonment. Torture. I would put none of these things past the Imminent Darkness and its so-called Citizen Law Enforcement.

My mother once told me that the Imminent Darkness feeds on fear and chaos. It likes disorder and destruction. These are the things that make it stronger. If fear could be a palpable thing, then I would be able to reach out and clench it in my fist.

Li's pace slows. The stench hits me first. Rot and sulfur. Is this the smell of death? I know as we near the hospital that Li is thinking the same thing as I am. Remembering Ahna's sallow skin and sunken in eyes. Her ragged breath and bloated belly. But that was the smell of one person's death. This is the smell of many. Hundreds. I start to cough, choking on the putrid odor. I pull my sweater up over my nose and mouth, but it's a futile gesture. Li does the same.

The hospital is set a little ways back from the rest of the colony. It's a building made of white stone and glass. You can only see looking out, but not looking in. Because of this, it reflects the red landscape, giving the building the appearance that it is that color itself. But it's not.

Once when I was about seven, the three of us—Ahna, Li, and myself—were swinging on the swings near our neighborhood. We were going higher and higher until Li had the brilliant idea that we should jump off the swing at its peak and see who could land the farthest. I remember him soaring through the air, as if he were made for flight, landing gracefully on both feet. Ahna had warned that it wasn't a good idea, but not to be outdone, I'd let go of the swing, urging my body forward into the air, feeling the chain link leave my sweaty fingers. I was flying—if only for a second—before I headed back toward the ground and realized I wasn't going to land gracefully on my feet like Li. I threw my hands down to break my fall, but in the process all of my weight landed on my left wrist.

My parents feared that I'd broken it and they'd taken me to the hospital. But I'd only badly sprained it. The only treatment was some ice and some anti-inflammatory medicine for a week or two. Li felt pretty sore after that. Although, I was never sure if he was sore because I got hurt or because Ahna was right or because I ruined his fun.

Tall lamp posts surround the hospital, making it look slightly inviting compared to other buildings in the colony. The landscaping is simple and well-manicured, shrubs and small trees line the walkways and there are matching benches on either side of the entrance.

As soon as you enter the hospital, there's a front desk. One hallway has a sliding door that leads to the emergency wing. The other hallway leads to the main lobby and a bank of elevators for different doctors' offices and patient rooms.

"How will we get past the front desk?" I ask. Li leads me toward the left where there's another drive that leads to the emergency vehicle entrance.

As if on cue, there's the sound of tires behind us. Li holds up his free arm and reveals a sleek, silver cuff. He pushes the button and he disappears before my eyes, but I can feel the solidness of his elbow still beneath my fingers.

We watch as an ambulance pulls up, red lights flashing. The side entrance to the hospital opens and a woman in white scrubs comes dashing out, a stethoscope hung around her neck. Her dark hair is pulled back in a ponytail. Pieces fall out around her face. She's wearing a mask around her nose and mouth.

"How many this time?" she asks a man who gets out of the passenger side of the ambulance, jogging to the back and pulling open the doors.

He wears a navy uniform, his sandy-colored hair is cut short. He too wears a mask over his mouth and nose.

"Three."

"Three?" the woman asks.

But it's a rhetorical question. She helps him get the door open then pulls a pair of latex gloves out of her shirt pocket and snaps them on. The man hands a small child to the nurse, she cradles her in her arms. The girl looks to be about six or seven. Even from here I can smell the death on her. She's wrapped in some sort of quilt, but her arm slips out, falling limply to her side, her skin jaundiced. The girl's head lolls to the right, and if we were actually visible, she'd be looking right at us, only her gaze is completely vacant. Huge, dilated pupils and purple-black circles beneath her eyes, blood at the corners of her mouth. Her hair is in braided pigtails and somehow that reminds me of Ahna.

The nurse sighs and presses the girl to her chest, running into the sliding doors of the emergency wing. The driver of the ambulance gets out and heads to the back of the ambulance to help his partner get the other two patients out. The first man emerges with a woman, guiding her carefully down the step at the back of the vehicle and toward the hospital entrance. Probably the girl's mother. She has on a ratty shawl. They pause as she's overcome with a fit of coughing, holding a tissue to her mouth. When she stops, and pulls it away I can see that it is covered with blood. The man urges her toward the entrance, and they're swallowed up by the brilliant, white light.

Finally, the driver emerges, guiding a man down the step. The man can barely stand on his own as the driver slams the back door of the ambulance shut. The driver catches the man as he stumbles, his knees buckling beneath his own weight. I assume it's the girl's father and the woman's husband. Li and I watch silently as the driver tries to lead the man toward the hospital entrance, but the man stumbles for a second time.

"Help! I need help out here!" The driver calls out. The man begins to cough and sputter, bloody spittle flying out of his mouth. His eyes roll back in his head and he begins to seize. The driver tries to gently hold his arms at his side, cradling him carefully. I feel as though my feet are glued to the spot, stuck with horror.

A new nurse comes running out of the emergency entrance. "We have a seizer!" she calls behind her as she covers the short distance to the two men.

But then the seizure stops as quickly as it began. Then nothing. The driver slides the man to the ground and begins chest compressions. But there is nothing. After an agonizing minute, the nurse calls the driver off. She pushes a button on a com she's wearing at her collar. "Get the coroner out to the emergency entrance."

"Copy," comes the garbled reply.

And that's it. The driver hangs his head, as if the man's death is somehow personally his fault.

The emergency door slides open and a large man with a white lab coat comes out with a gurney. He picks up the newly dead man as if he is a child's ragdoll, weighing nothing at all. The man is all skin and bones, his chin and mouth bloody. Vacant eyes staring at nothing. The coroner puts a blanket over the man, a pointless gesture because the dead do not know the kindness extended by the living. The nurse and the coroner push the gurney back in through the hospital doors, leaving the ambulance driver alone, still kneeling as if he can't believe what has just happened.

Suddenly, he begins to cough, loud hacking coughs that shake his entire body. He pulls at the face mask in frustration, and when he pulls it away I can see that it is spotted with blood. His shoulders begin to shake with silent sobs. I feel sick. Torn between what I've just seen and wanting to offer this man whose just been given his death sentence some semblance of comfort.

Something catches my eye, just past his shoulder and I feel Li's body tense beside me because he sees it too. A pair of yellow eyes between the black tree trunks. They stare at us then disappear, dissolving into the shadows.

I have seen enough. I came looking for answers. And I now know what I must do.

CHAPTER 23

Li says that I do not have to do this alone. But he does not know what I have to do. What I must to do to save everyone that I love. We eat dinner around a long, wooden table that's carved with wear.

Bax smiles and laughs. He's actually very witty and I can easily see why he and Sloan are friends. Doran and Bax banter back and forth and I'm reminded of the first few times I saw Doran, a seemingly permanent scowl on his face. His easy smile and caring nature that was hidden beneath the surface took a while to crack, but I'm thankful that I was the one to help crack it. Cerise sits with her shoulder pressed against Li's, smiling whenever he leans close and whispers in her ear. Sloan's hand rests on my thigh beneath the table as he periodically joins in the conversation. I may never see them again. There's the possibility that I could die, but if I don't do this there's the possibility *they* will die. It's an easy choice when you look at it like that. *A decision will be made that cannot be undone.*

I pick at my food, pushing it around my plate. Some overcooked meat and undercooked potatoes. Sloan notices, his brow furrowed, but he doesn't say anything.

Later that evening, I slip a note into Li's pants pocket. It tells him not to do anything stupid, definitely not to break Cerise's heart, and, oh yeah, by the way you're immortal. Now, Sloan sleeps beside me his breath slow and even against the back of my neck. I slip carefully from beneath his arm and begin to put on my boots. I'm reaching for my messenger bag when I feel a firm hand grab my forearm.

I turn. Sloan looks at me with very alert eyes.

"Please. Don't." And it's all I can manage to say. Because if I say anything more it will be the undoing of me. Of everything.

"Kata. Let me go with you." His voice is gruff with worry. I can feel the quickening of the pulse in his fingertips which are wrapped around my arm.

"I. I can't." Tears well-up in my eyes and I brush at them stubbornly with my free hand. It would have been so much easier if he'd been asleep.

He sits up and pulls me toward him. I land in his lap and he wraps his arms around me. His mouth is somewhere between my neck and ear. "I took a vow. And I may have taken it blindly before, but I've honored it again and again since I've known you. I am to protect you until your last breath. Until the end."

I close my eyes and wonder if he can feel the hammering of my heart—my screwed up half-immortal heart. "Some things you can't protect me from," I whisper and turn in his arms so that I'm facing him, our chins almost touching.

"Then let me be with you. Let me stay with you." He leans in and kisses me slowly. "Let me be there with you no matter what happens. For better or for worse. In life and in death. An everlasting vow is just that. Everlasting." He kisses me again, pressing me into him as if he could merge his body with mine. If he's trying to convince me. It works. But I wonder if I will regret it later.

"Okay," I whisper. "Come with me." This time I grab the collar of his shirt and kiss him with the possibility of all the kisses we might never have.

. . .

The leaves crunch beneath our boots. I decided the forest is the best place. It's away from the colony and it's away from the tent city. We could go out to the perimeter, but we'd be unprotected and out in the open. Sloan says nothing as we reach the metal star. It's the star I asked Doran to make for Ahna's grave. It still looks new, gleaming silver in the moonlight. There are some smudges of paint and some nail holes on the pieces because it was scrap metal, but it's beautiful nonetheless. It's nailed to the tree where Ahna died. At first I thought the idea might be a bit morbid, to mark the place of something so gruesome. So wrong. But then I thought it wasn't fair that someone so beautiful and so young, should just fade away like a dream.

Sloan's hand hasn't left mine since we left. Now he removes it to put an arm around my shoulder. Pulling me in close. His jacket smells like leather, his hair and skin like soap and the sea.

"Tell me," he finally says.

I pull my messenger bag over my head and drop it on the ground. I pull the Metal stone and the crystal from my pants pocket.

"Two stones. But only one needs destroyed." I hold up the Metal stone. "This stone can manipulate the energy of all Metals. If I destroy it, it will literally change every Metal that we know. All the darkness will be pushed out of them. It will return my Metal to me and I will be stronger."

"But?"

"But it might not be enough to defeat the Imminent Darkness. I could still lose. The ID is timeless and ancient. It's wiser. And…I'm not sure I have the right to change people without their permission."

Sloan nods. "Fair enough." He gestures to the crystal. "And that?"

I hold it up, glinting in the moonlight. "If I destroy the crystal, it will have no effect on the energetic make-up of the Metal Elementals. It will also seal off the Elemental Abyss and close Xon 9 off from all the other lands. According to Bina, if that happens the Imminent Darkness will be vanquished for good. Cast out into the black hole of the Universe. Or something like that."

He sighs and asks again, "But?"

I take a deep, shaky breath. "But I will never be able to see my mother and father again. Bina said transport objects will no longer work. And, she may have mentioned that it could kill me. Even though I'm half-immortal I think that my mortality is somehow linked to the Elemental Abyss. She said some things she can't see. And this is one of them."

Sloan takes the news surprisingly well. "And did you think it was braver if you were to die alone? More honorable?"

"No. I just." I turn toward the metal star. "No one should have to watch someone they love die."

"And no one—*especially* someone you love—should have to die alone." He puts his arms around my waist and pulls me into him, pressing his forehead against mine. "I love you, Ka Waylon. And I am willing to suffer the pain of watching you possibly take your last breath, if it means that you are not alone. Because I will not choose to remember that moment. Instead, I will remember the kindness of your words, the sparkle in your chocolate eyes, the scent of crushed flowers and ocean breezes in your hair, the softness of your lips pressed against mine. The fire in your heart." He kisses my forehead before releasing me.

He unsheathes the jewel-encrusted dagger and hands it to me. "I will stay with you to the end."

"No matter what?" The question comes out shakily. I take the dagger and it feels cold and heavy in my hands.

"No matter what."

No lies.

I kneel in the dirt at the base of the tree. Ahna's tree. Sloan kneels across from me and I hand him the Metal stone. He rubs his thumb across it, then drops it into the pocket of his jacket. I have to admire that he didn't ask me to rethink my choice. We may love one another, but I am one person. The crystal could save hundreds, possibly thousands. I lay the crystal down in the dirt before me. It winks at me like a fallen star.

Tears push out and roll slowly down my cheeks. You think you will be brave in the face of potential death. That you will face death like a hero. But my insides feel hollow. There's so much that I want to do, so much that I suddenly want to say. But I am an abomination. When the Universe was created, someone like me wasn't meant to exist. The daughter of a mortal and immortal, a grandchild to the Universe. And maybe this is the chance for the Universe to balance itself. It's the chance for me to make things right again.

I pull the dagger back near my shoulder. It's important that the crystal shatter. I look up at Sloan. His green eyes are stormy seas.

"I love you," I manage, but it comes out garbled as I continue to silently cry. This is not noble. This does not feel like a hero's death. It feels unfair and I feel rotten for thinking it. Part of me knows I may not die, but the other part of me fears what may happen if I don't.

Sloan reaches across the space between us and takes my free hand.

"Together."

"Together," I echo. I take a deep breath and pull the dagger back. I will not close my eyes. I will meet my fate with my eyes wide open. I slice the dagger through the air, making a clean arc as the steel tip finds the surface of the crystal and it shatters into thousands of tiny pieces.

At first nothing seems to happen except my heart pounding in my chest. And then I hear it. I hear it howling for me, calling my name on the wind.

"Kaaaaaaaaaaaaaaaaaataaaaaaaaaaaaaaaaa."

The howling grows louder and I can feel something cold suddenly reach inside me, like the hand of a corpse. Right through my chest. Through my heart. Death itself. It fills my blood, which once ran like Fire, and turns it to ice. Silencing it. I let out a moan and feel myself fall backward. Black smoke writhes around my body. Smoke? No. I see the flash of yellow. No, not Death. The Imminent Darkness. It wraps itself around my wrists and my arms, pinning them to my sides. I try to kick, but it entwines itself around my feet. It's everywhere.

I can feel Sloan's presence and hear his voice. But it seems very far away, as if he's talking to me from underwater. The dark cloud continues to squeeze itself around me, wrapping tighter and tighter, like a boa constrictor killing its meal before it devours it. I can feel the grit in my eyes and in my mouth as I try to yell Sloan's name. This is the choice I made.

"Such a shame? Isn't it? A young, pretty thing like yourself." The voice of an old man whispers in my ear. I thrash at the words.

"You knew. Either way you would win." I don't have to say the words. I just think them. "You would either destroy the colony and everything around me. Or you would destroy me."

"At the cost of also destroying myself," the ancient voice purrs. "But yes, I suppose it is as you say. A win-win situation."

The coldness moves through my body, spreading across my chest and into my head. In the Land of Wood, Sloan and I saw snow. I fell into an icy lake. And that is what this feels like now. As if ice is moving through my veins, encompassing my body.

"Where I go, you go, Impossible Girl."

My heartbeat slows down and the edges of my vision are becoming fuzzy. I hear muffled voices, but can't make them out. Are they voices of the dead? Or of the living? My teeth begin to chatter and my body trembles. One death for the lives of hundreds. Maybe you don't have to be brave to be a hero. Maybe it's simply knowing the right thing and doing it. I let out a sigh and close my eyes. I will no longer fight my fate. I let images of Sloan drift through my mind as it slowly begins to shut down. His beautiful silver-green scales. The hint of an impish smile. Eyes calm as the sea. A single kiss worth so many unspoken words. I welcome death as my body finally freezes and my heart goes still.

CHAPTER 24

Death is not what I expected it to be. In fact, death sounds a lot like Bina.

"Don't just stand there, ye Big Oaf! More blankets from the ovens!" I hear a commotion and the sound of boots running. A few seconds later something warm is draped over my body. My teeth are chattering and I can feel my arms and legs shivering. More warm things are draped over me. My eyes feel gritty and I try to open my mouth to speak, but it feels like it's stuffed full of cotton.

"What about a tincture?" A familiar female voice asks.

"They're already gathering ingredients. Some of them can only be found in the mountains," replies Bina.

"What if we run out of time?" asks a male voice. Doran, I think. He sounds far away, like we're playing a game of telephone with two plastic cups and a string through the bottoms.

"Well, then time will have to wait." For the first time I notice a big hand clasped around mine. It's the single spot of warmth I can feel across my whole body. My lips try to smile, but I'm not sure if the thought makes it through my nervous system to tell my mouth what to do.

Sloan.

Until the end. No matter what.

. . .

I dream of the Land of Earth. My mother with her chestnut curls shining in the sun as she sits in her garden. She's reading a book and my father sits beside her also reading a book and sipping a cup of tea. The smell of gardenia, rose, and jasmine itches my nose. I am hidden behind green vines and the wooden posts of the pergola.

My mother looks up as if she hears something. "Absalom? Did you hear that?"

"What's that dear?" My father draws his eyes away from his book and follows my mother's gaze.

And for the briefest of moments, my parents are looking right at me.

"Oh. Oh, dear!" My mother's fingers fling to her mouth and her gray eyes fill with tears. Her face is so young and my father looks so old beside her. Two lovers, one frozen in time, one victim to time.

My father sees me. "You are so brave. So beautifully, vibrantly brave, my love." He reaches across the space over the little side table, and grabs my mother's hand.

"We love you, Kata. We understand the choice you made. And we love you." My mother's chest seems to swell with something like pride. It wasn't long ago that a choice I made threw our lives into chaos. It feels good to have somehow righted something that was wrong.

I raise my hand to wave good-bye, but the dream is already slipping away and into something new.

. . .

I'm in the Land of Wood inside the trunk of a hollowed tree. Nahele. I smile. The dining hall is loud and raucous with singing and dancing. There's the clink of glasses and the clatter of plates. I spot a brown-haired fairy dancing with a blonde-haired warrior. The keeper of the Genesis. The fairy—Hennie—points over Qildor's shoulder at me, her hazel eyes sparkling. Qildor's pale brown eyes find me and he frowns, tilting his head slightly. I wave and they wave back, confused. Before I can explain, I'm whisked away again.

. . .

There's a vast gray sea all around me. I'm sitting in a little wooden boat, rocking idly back and forth. A splash beside me startles me, droplets of water landing into the bottom of my boat. I lean over and peer into the sea.

"Didn't think I'd see you here, Princess." Black hair and a scaled face look back at me.

"Brooks?" I ask. My mouth still feels like it's full of cotton, and the words come out as if I'm not used to speaking them.

"In the flesh. Or something like that." His webbed fingers grip the side of the boat.

"But you. I thought you were dead. The Elemental Abyss…" I try to erase the sight of the dead Unbalanced Waters lining the shore of the enchanted lake from my memory.

"Like I said. Something like that." He flips his tail, sending more water into my boat.

"Where am I?"

"Here. There. Everywhere. It was nice of you to visit though." His voice is cheerful.

"Are you a ghost?" I ask. I reach out and touch one of his green fingers.

"Do you believe in ghosts?"

I shake my head. "No."

"Well, then I can't be one, can I?" He grins, revealing sharp-pointed teeth.

"I thought I'd never see you again." I place my hand over his. Brooks saved my life more times than I'd care to admit.

"And yet here you are. But I think our time is almost up, Princess." He looks up at the blue sky overheard. But I don't see anything.

"Did I come here for something?" I ask, suddenly confused. As if I am forgetting something very important.

"I'm really sorry to do this to you. Really, I am. But you'll thank me later. One word of advice though: breathe!" And with that he forces the side of the boat down and I tumble out, splashing into the cool water.

I've never been a good swimmer. I thrash around and Brooks is nowhere to be found. How convenient. My vision begins to go black. What had he said? I'll thank him later. *Yeah, right.* No, something else. The wisp of it is so close I can almost make it out. Oh, that's right.

Breathe.

I take in a big gulp, salty water rushing in, filling my insides. Pushing out the coldness. The salt melting the ice that fills my veins. Warmth begins to creep in. Sweet, life. Heat. Voices. My eyes fling open and I gasp, taking in a deep breath of life-giving air. My free hand flings to my chest, where it finds my heart pounding rapidly. My beating, very much alive heart.

I'm alive.

Chapter 25

"She's awake!" Sloan is on his feet, his hand still clutching mine like a tether. He kisses the top of my head.

I'm unsure of using words. My lips taste like salt. So instead, I look around. I'm on a cot inside a tent. Not my bed. Not my tent. There are shelves with glasses and jars lining the walls. A lantern hangs at the tent's apex. There are heavy blankets tossed over me. There's a wooden chair beside the bed, with a hoodie draped over it.

Footsteps grow louder and several people burst through the tent, eyes bright and out of breath. Li stumbles over to the cot and throws his arms across me, kissing my cheeks with cool lips—as if he'd just come from outside. Cerise stands behind him and behind her Doran, they're all wearing relieved expressions.

"Give the girl some breathin' room. Get outta the way." Bina elbows her way past the others, but she doesn't move Sloan who finally sits back down in the chair beside the bed.

"Gave us quite the scare, Kata," Bina says. She brushes a wrinkled hand along my forehead and down my cheek. She pauses at the curve in my neck. "Good. A strong pulse." She continues taking inventory of my vital signs.

"Here." Sloan hands me a warm glass of water that smells like honey. I take a grateful sip. It's smooth all the way down, dispelling the cotton that lines my throat. After several more sips and once Bina has relented, I finally ask the obvious question.

"Why am I not dead?"

The others exchange glances that clearly say, *Oh boy.*

"You were dead," Li replies.

Cerise slaps him on the shoulder. "We talked about this. *Tact,* remember?"

"Oh, right. You may or may not have been dead," he corrects.

Cerise sighs. "What he means to say is, we weren't sure what was happening. Your vitals all slowed and were all but non-existent. If it weren't for Sloan's quick thinking…surely, you wouldn't be here with us now."

"Not the Metal stone! Sloan, tell me you didn't destroy the Metal stone!" I cry gripping his hand and pulling him toward me.

He fumbles in his pocket and pulls out the smooth hematite stone. I let out a sigh, falling back onto the pillow.

"No, but you had these. In your bag." He pulls out a packet of matches with a siren on it and the words: The Old Tavern and the

Sea.

I shake my head. "I don't understand."

He slips the matches back into his pocket. And entwines his fingers with mine. "I saw it. When it came for you. The Imminent Darkness. I saw it wrap itself around you, choking you. I'm not my mother, but I am my mother's son. I clawed through your bag, hoping you hadn't thrown out the remaining matches. Luckily, you hadn't. I found them and I used them to set the pieces of the crystal on fire. I didn't know if it would save you, but I figured what was worse than death"?

He rubs his thumb slowly back and forth over the back of my hand. "The energy from the crystal, it grew stronger and it pulled the smoke—the Imminent Darkness—into the pieces. The flame went from orange to blue to purple to green. It screamed as it went, a blood-piercing scream so loud that it drew the others."

"It ain't easy for something that ancient to be destroyed," Bina acknowledges.

"Then the strangest thing happened, the tree—Ahna's tree— seemed to pull the crystal pieces up and into itself, like a mini tornado, lodging the pieces into its trunk."

"Ahna?" I look at Li, expecting sadness but his brown eyes are filled with joy not sorrow.

"And then I saw you lying there. Your skin was tinged blue and you were shaking horribly. I knew I had to get you warm, so I picked you up and wrapped you inside my coat. I carried you all the way back. I think you might know the rest."

"How long?" I ask.

"Five days," Sloan says softly. "I wasn't sure...I thought maybe..."

"You saved me. Ahna saved me. Oh, moons." I press Sloan's hand against my cheek, feeling its warmth. That's why I was at all those places. I was hanging in between the lands of the living and the dead.

"Alright, now. I think she's in good hands," Bina says, ushering the others out. Before leaving, she turns to Sloan, "Not too long, Son. She needs rest." She pats him on the shoulder before disappearing out the tent, the flap closing behind her.

As soon as she's gone, Sloan removes some of the extra blankets so I won't get too warm and crawls into the cot beside me. I turn so that our foreheads are pressed together, our clasped hands in between us.

"I thought you were dead," he whispers. "I was so afraid. Your heart beat was so slow that it almost wasn't. I wondered if I'd made a terrible mistake."

"I thought I was dead," I whisper back. "I saw things. My parents. Hennie and Qildor. Brooks. Brooks is the one who told me to breathe. That's when I woke up."

He nuzzles my cheek. "Well, then I'm thankful he was there. Wherever there was."

I snuggle in closer to him, his body heat staving off the lingering chill. "Me too." I have so many questions. What's happened in the last five days? Is the Leadership Council back in control—or at least

Esmeralda? Has the spread of *cassusmortem* ceased? But fatigue wins the battle and my eyelids slide closed. I fall into a peaceful sleep, wrapped in the arms of my protector.

...

I carry a box into the living room of Sloan's house. Now that my parents aren't ever coming back, there's truly no reason to keep a vacant house. I set the box on the table and flop onto the couch beside Sloan. He grins and pulls my legs into his lap.

When the Imminent Darkness was destroyed, the *cassusmoretem* stopped spreading. People began to heal, recovering in only a couple of days' time. They went back to their homes, some with loved one-sized holes in their hearts. The New Council held a memorial service in memory of the lives that were lost to the Empty Death.

The Citizen Law Enforcement—without the influence of the Imminent Darkness's dark energy—are temporarily in prison, awaiting trial for their crimes. A fair trial that will be judged by the New Council, which Esmeralda established, not including herself, but allowing each Elemental to nominate a representative to serve in five year terms. No one, except Esmeralda, will ever know the extent to which the Leadership Council was involved with the Imminent Darkness, but for now the statue in front of Council Hall has been razed, to be replaced with something new. Ideas were open to submission, and Doran submitted an entry for a metal sculpture of a teenage girl with a heart fractured into five pieces. He called it the Impossible Girl. And it won.

I run my hand along the back of my neck, feeling the smooth

skin of my tattoo. It's different now. Just plain old ink on plain old skin. Bina explained to me that most likely when I destroyed the crystal and closed the Elemental Abyss forever, my gifts went right along with it. The only evidence of what used to be is a thin scar on the inside of either wrist. But that's okay. I don't need to see the future or be able to tell when people are lying in order to feel whole again. As a wise guy once told me, some people liked me just the way I was.

Sloan slips off my boots and begins to massage my feet. With the money I got from selling my parents' house I was able to buy Bina and Finn a new trailer in the Black Bazaar. I don't think Bina's going to be telling any more fortunes any time soon. I think she'll be sticking more to the herbal remedies and tinctures, especially for any lingering side effects of *cassusmortem*. Meanwhile, Finn has accepted the Metal Elementals' nomination for the New Council. I don't think they could have selected a braver, more kind person.

We haven't heard from Michaela, but last I heard she was switched to pushing papers in a military office, no longer working in intelligence. Guess, that's what happens when you let the colony's most wanted fugitive get away.

Bax has opened a training facility in the Black Bazaar. He says the military life is over for him, but he still finds enjoyment in training people in hand to hand combat, who want to learn. It seems really popular. I guess after what happened, people always want to be prepared. Apparently, Zora is one of his best customers.

"Hey, hey!" I'd left the front door open and Cerise sticks her red head in, followed by Li. Li has a quiver over his shoulder. "We were just going for some shooting practice at Bax's, and thought we'd drop in and see if you need help with anything?"

"No. We're good. But if you guys want to come over later, I hear Sloan is an excellent cook!" I grin.

"Great. Make double. Shooting always makes me hungry." Li says tapping his quiver.

Cerise rolls her eyes. "Just breathing makes you hungry. Okay, see you later!" They disappear closing the door behind them.

Li never mentioned the note I left him. And I'm not even sure if it's still true, but I have the strong suspicion that any immortality—half or not—was tied to the Elemental Abyss. It sealing has restored the balance of the Universe. I may not be able to see my parents again, but I know that they're both only a dream away. I spin the turquoise ring around my index finger.

Sloan stops rubbing my feet and takes my hand. "You made the right choice."

I wiggle my toes. "I know. It even *feels* right." I look around the small bungalow, some framed pictures of my parents on a dresser, Sloan's jeweled dagger hanging on the wall as a reminder of our extraordinary adventures.

"It does, doesn't it?" He smiles, lifting my hand to his lips and planting a kiss on my palm.

Ordinary never felt so good

ABOUT THE AUTHOR

Jennifer L. Kelly is a middle childhood educator. She resides in Cleveland, Ohio. When she isn't writing, she can be found fangirling over *Doctor Who*, doing yoga, spending time with her dog, taking photos for her #bookstagram, or making candles for her Etsy shop: TheBookishFlame. This is her second series for young adults. Her first novel, *The Prophecy: The Lucia Chronicles Book 1*, was published in January 2014. Visit her website **Skim.Scheme.Scribble:** **www.jenniferlkelly.com** Or say *HI!* :

✉ **info@jenniferlkelly.com**

🐦 **JenniferLKelly3**

👍 **AuthorJenniferLKelly**

📷 **AuthorJenniferLKelly**

ACKNOWLEDGEMENTS

There are many people who supported me on this journey. Always first is my Dad who beta reads, edits, and brainstorms with me on all of my books. But just as important are my Advanced Readers who I found on #bookstagram. These ladies in particular stuck with me for the long haul: Alex, Beth, Britta, Daisy, Ella, JaNae, Ksandra, Izzy, Michelle, Nica, and Nichelle! Thank you for being anything but ordinary! I'd like to thank the artists that have worked on this series with me. The better than I ever dreamed Elemental Star by Joshua Jadon, the gorgeous map created by Rebecca Solow that helped both Ka and me to find our way, and to the amazingly talented Lesya at Blackbird Ink for creating my OTP art. Thank you all from the bottom of my humbly ordinary heart!

COMING SOON...

Fall 2017

www.ingramcontent.com/pod-product-compliance
Lightning Source LLC
Chambersburg PA
CBHW022149170626
46807CB00005B/2129